TURN OF THE TIDE

They had stolen the ranch that Lee Standish had sweated blood to build.

They had dirtied the name that Lee Standish had always kept clean.

They had put a price on Lee Standish's head and a kill-crazy mob on his trail.

They had beaten Lee Standish to a bloody pulp and tossed his trussed-up, weighted-down body into a flood-swollen creek.

But they had made a mistake.

They had left life in Lee Standish's body and death in his trigger finger. . . .

Also by Charles N. Heckelmann and available from Popular Library:

HARD MAN WITH A GUN
BULLET LAW
LAWLESS RANGE
HELL IN HIS HOLSTERS
LET THE GUNS ROAR
TWO-BIT RANCHER
SIX-GUN OUTCAST
TRUMPETS IN THE DAWN

Charles N. Heckelmann

VENGEANCE TRAIL

POPULAR LIBRARY • NEW YORK

Published by Popular Library, CBS Publications,
CBS Consumer Publishing, a Division of CBS Inc., by
arrangement with the author

August, 1977

ISB[illegible]5-04031-9

PRINTED IN THE UNITED STATES OF AMERICA

Chapter One

Shouldering through the front door of the Circle B ranchhouse, Lee Standish strode into an ugly, strained silence. One moment, while his boots drummed solidly across the broad veranda, the murmur of voices had reached him distinctly. The next moment all conversation ceased and a feeling of strain and hostility washed across the room.

Every one of the cowmen in that room looked up at his entrance, and in every pair of eyes Lee Standish detected the bright flicker of doubt and mistrust and a rising unfriendliness.

They were all here: Brad Buchan of the Circle B; Chad Runyan of the Double R; John Noonan of the Diamond N; a few other smaller hill ranchers; Adam Brill, president of the Drayton bank, as well as owner of the AB Connected, a small cow ranch adjoining the Double R. In addition, Jess Hawley, a government weather bureau expert visiting with Brill, stood by himself in a corner.

Brad Buchan detached himself from the others and faced Standish with a brittle displeasure showing in his eyes. He was a towering hulk of a man, thick in the shoulders and arms, with a heavy, jutting jaw and narrow blue eyes.

"Nobody invited yuh here," said Buchan. "There's the door. Don't slam it as you go out."

Standish shook his head, an iron resolve showing in his face.

"I reckon I'll stay. When I found out about the meetin' I figgered it was my place as a cattleman to be here."

Watching the other men in the room, Standish saw no break in their expressions, and anger began to have its way with him.

He was a tall, wide-shouldered man in his late twenties with somber gray eyes wide-set in a craggy face. His skin was deeply bronzed; his jaw was square and firm and there were tiny weather wrinkles at the corners of his eyes.

A mop of dark hair formed a thick cowl across his forehead where it fell away from a tilted-back coffee-brown Stetson. Chocolate-colored bullhide chaps, cut Cheyenne fashion, draped his powerful legs, which were encased in tall-heeled black boots. A single cartridge belt was looped about his slender waist, the hand-tooled leather holster snugging a worn, ivory-butted Colt.

"Knowin' how yuh feel about our nester neighbors I didn't figger yuh'd be any help in organizing for action," stated Buchan. "We aim to put an end to all the trouble we've been havin' lately. Rustlers have been raidin' our stock and Chad Runyan had several haystacks burned t'other night."

"Not to mention a couple of butchered cows," put in Chad Runyan, a slender, lean-waisted man, lithe and catlike in all his movements.

He had a rugged, clean-shaven face. His sharp blue eyes were as bleak as his countenance, and his mouth was a thin stubborn gash.

"I've had the same trouble," Standish reminded them. "When I find out who them rustlers are me and the boys will drive 'em out."

"If yuh're after those raiders yuh don't have to look any further than Jube Rockett and his sodbuster pals," growled Buchan, a dull savagery pinching his features. "They're the only jaspers who'd butcher cows for meat.

I figger they've banded together to steal our beef because me and Runyan here warned them to clear off that government range."

"The only way to handle the nesters," cut in Runyan, his narrow mouth settling in a determined line, "is to force them out with guns."

A murmur of approval ran around the room, but the attention of all was centered upon Lee Standish.

"My advice to all of yuh," said Standish slowly, "is not to go off half-cocked. We don't *know* the nesters are behind the trouble we've been havin'. I've lost as many critters as any of yuh, but I don't aim to do any shootin' until I know I'm shootin' at the guilty parties."

"What kind of a cowman are yuh, Standish?" demanded Buchan, a broad flare to his nostrils. "Yuh seem mighty interested in jaspers that are a cowman's natural enemies. Rockett and the other plow-pushers are usin' range that belongs to us. They've got no right to it."

"They've as much right there as we have."

"It's our land," insisted Chad Runyan.

"Only by right of usage." There was an impatient note in Standish's voice. "If people want to settle there we can't stop them, especially since the government opened it for homesteading."

An ominous silence flattened through the room again. Buchan's eyes blazed in fury. Runyan's mouth thinned out.

"We can stop 'em with our guns!" fumed Brad Buchan. "I suggest we give 'em one more chance to vamose. If they refuse we'll see they all go out on the flat of their backs."

"Now yuh're talkin'," said Runyan. "I'm all for that."

"What do you say? Are yuh with us?" Buchan asked Standish.

"No," snapped Standish stubbornly. "I'll stay on the

fence until I'm sure the nesters really are guilty of what yuh say."

Buchan sneered, his lips curling against his yellowed teeth.

"There'll be no straddlin' the fence in this fight that's comin'. Yuh're either for or against us."

A grim barrier as solid as a wall seemed to have sprung up between Lee Standish and his neighbors.

"Yuh've got my answer," he said. "Just remember this. If you use force to make the nesters clear out yuh'll be steppin' outside the law."

"To blazes with the law!" shouted Chad Runyan, his eyes fever-bright. "We'll make our own law to protect ourselves."

A bold insolence came into Buchan's face. He was tough and hard and knew it and wanted others to know it as well. It showed in his flashing eyes, in his booming voice.

"It ought to be as plain as the nose on yore face why you weren't invited to this meetin'," grunted Buchan. "For a cowman yuh're all-fired sympathetic with the nesters—especially since yuh've been hangin' around that nester gal, Sally Rockett. It wouldn't surprise me if yuh were workin' with the nesters against Runyan and the rest of us."

Lamplight cast its flickering glow upon Standish. There was something stern and very compelling about him. He was a man inured to this wild land's close and hard risks, a man not to be trifled with. There had never been much laughter in him, and now the taciturn hardness of his unyielding shape got to all these men, upsetting their confidence.

"Buchan, it seems to me yuh're so anxious to start a war between the nesters and the cattlemen that you might be the one responsible for all the trouble we've been havin'," Standish snapped harshly.

The Circle B owner's eyes turned hard and searching.

"Why, yuh blasted nester lover!" he fumed, leaping back and plunging his long arms toward the holstered guns at his thighs.

His splayed fingers curled around the wooden butts, dragged the shining weapons half clear of leather, then halted as Standish's single ivory-handled Colt flicked into his fist in a matical blur of speed, then centered on Buchan's chest.

There was something dark and deadly in the unwavering gun muzzle, in the sibilant swiftness of that draw. But more than that, the half-wild, implacable look in Standish's eyes stopped Buchan as if he'd butted into a stone wall. He stood entirely unmoving, his hands arrested, his breathing quick and shallow, a sullen anger oiling his features.

"Don't ever draw iron against me, Buchan," warned Standish in cold flat tones, "unless yuh're fixin' to finish the job in gunsmoke."

Soomeone's boots scraped along the floor, and the sound of Standish cocking his gun was a brittle murmur, tugging at everyone's nerves.

"Another thing, Brad," he said, "yuh're so anxious to gun the nesters outa the valley that I mean to watch yuh. I'm a cowman like the rest of yuh, but the nesters have a right to live. As long as they've settled on land that don't belong to us, I don't see where we can do anythin' about it."

Even while he talked Standish could feel the hot pulsations of anger and mistrust that flowed back and forth across the room. He'd crossed a bridge tonight. He saw that quite clearly. From now on he would be an outcast among the cattlemen. There was no faith, no warmth for him here.

It irritated him, touched his mind with a hint of despair, yet nothing could have made him take back the things he had said. Regretting the advent of the nesters, the plowing up of good grazing land as any cowman would, he could not bring himself to move against them until he had found a sufficient reason for doing so. Until then he meant to stay on the fence no matter what the cost to himself in lost friendship and esteem. He had his own ideals, his concepts of right and wrong and meant to live by them.

Ignoring Brad Buchan's guns and the harsh, unyielding threat revealed in the angry faces about him, Lee Standish holstered his Colt.

"I'm leavin' now," Standish informed the gathering. "And if yuh're wise yuh'll wait for definite proof before makin' any move."

"Get out!" flared Brad Buchan, his big hands clenching and unclenching at his sides. "If you like the sodbusters so much, go to the basin and live with 'em. That's where you belong!"

A white flame of anger flickered in Standish's somber gray eyes. He turned from the door and not a man in that room missed the rash destructiveness in him at that moment. He took one step toward Buchan when the smooth tones of Adam Brill halted him.

"Hold on, Lee. We don't want any killing here. You and Buchan are both mad and don't know what you're saying." Buchan growled his contradiction of that and Standish, his eyes meeting Brill's without friendliness, turned wordlessly back to the door. "Wait, Lee. While yuh're here I want to tell yuh about yore note."

Standish's thick, dark eyebrows lifted and he spoke hastily.

"I'll see yuh about that tomorrow."

Adam Brill shook his head.

"We can settle the matter now. I can't renew it, Lee."

In spite of the stiff rigidity of his tall, sinewy frame

Lee Standish was momentarily disturbed. A hint of dismay came into his cheeks, then vanished as his eyes sought the banker.

Adam Brill was a thick-set mild-mannered man with a pale-cheeked face. His eyes were gray-green and oddly fathomless. He dressed like a gambler in white broadcloth shirt, black string tie and neatly pressed black trousers and frock coat.

"Did yuh have to mention it in front of everybody?" demanded Standish. A shadow crossed his face and the old headlong temper was crowding him again. "Or mebbe yuh planned it that way so Buchan and Runyan and the others would have a chance to crow over me."

A sudden brilliance flamed in Brill's eyes, then was gone.

"Yuh're angry, Lee," he murmured, "so I'll overlook it."

"Did yuh forget yuh promised me an extension on the note yuh hold on my outfit if I ever needed it?" Standish went on relentlessly.

"I know, but conditions have changed."

"So?" Blood was rushing through Standish's head. "How come yuh gave renewals to some o' the hill ranchers right in this room?"

Brill flushed uncomfortably, but his manner remained unruffled.

"That was two months ago. Things have tightened up since then. I'd like to help yuh, but—"

"Why don't yuh say what's in yore mind—that yuh won't give me a renewal because yuh'd like to add my spread to yores and a good way to do it is through foreclosure proceedings?" Standish fumed. "Mebbe yore friends don't know about the ridiculous offer yuh made me for the ranch two weeks ago."

For a moment Brill's composure left him and hate rolled wickedly in his narrowing eyes.

"Yuh seem to be primed for trouble, Lee," the banker murmured, the words issuing from him with evident effort, "so let me give yuh a little warning. Don't set yoreself against all yore neighbors. Don't let yore sympathies for the nesters warp yore sense of values. The cowmen can't trust yuh now and the nesters won't trust yuh. Think that over."

"I have," snapped Standish, "and my decision stands."

Brill shook his head dolefully. His face showed a hint of concern, but there was something odd and strange in his gray-green eyes.

"I'm afraid yuh're headed for grief then."

Standish remained unmoved. He was altogether lonely with his thoughts gray and hard, but his resolutions unchanged.

"Well, I'm not one to back down from trouble when it comes my way," he murmured, and no voice was ever so soft, yet so definitely implacable.

Then he was turning from them and shouldering through the door. For a moment no one stirred and no one spoke while they listened to the run of his horse pounding across the yard.

The white stallion Lee Standish rode was laboring when he skidded to a halt in the front yard of his own Falling S spread. There hadn't been any reason for haste. But the anger and the bitterness in him had impelled him to take refuge in a wild burst of speed.

Somehow he felt no warmth when he saw the butter-yellow path of brilliance flushing from the bunkhouse windows.

"That you, Lee?" called a voice out of the shadows.

"Yeah."

A man moved away from the bunkhouse and came across the yard. Standish cast a swift glance toward the barn and corrals, then dismounted and entered the combined living room and office at the front of the house.

After he had lit a lamp he turned to face Ed Gorevin, his foreman, who clumped into the room after him.

A cluster of large round freckles was the first thing you noticed about the Falling S ramrod. They covered all of his blunt, square face, matching the color of his heavy-lidded eyes. His nose was flat, his lips long and thin. He was a homely man with legs bowed from years spent in the saddle and a hard cast to his face.

"How did yuh make out, Lee?" he inquired.

"I didn't," was the curt reply. "Buchan, Runyan and all the rest are dead set on runnin' the nesters outa the basin."

Gorevin clucked his agreement, his eyes roundly appraising Standish and noting his displeasure.

"That's the only way we'll ever stop the rustlin' and beef butcherin'," the ramrod declared bluntly. "Nobody'll ever make me believe those masked raiders that've been plaguin' us are anythin' but nesters."

"Yuh're wrong," said Standish, a flicker of annoyance crossing his bronzed countenance. "The nesters are family men and wouldn't go in for anythin' like that. The raiders are either outlaws or some cowman's paid hirelings set on startin' a range war so their leader can mop us and profit after it's all over."

A disbelieving smile cracked Gorevin's freckled features.

"What about the note?" he inquired.

"Brill refuses to grant an extension so we'll have to market a beef herd if we aim to hold on to the Falling S."

"It can't be done!" A dismal conviction colored Gorevin's talk. "There isn't time. That note has only a week to run. It'd take that long to comb the brakes and canyons and make a decent gather, let alone haze the critters all the way to railhead at New Benton."

Standish's face was dark with brooding thoughts, but

now his chin lifted with a determination Gorevin knew so well.

"We're doin' it," he said, dry-voiced, "if we have to work night and day without sleep. Rout out the crew now. Tell the cook to load up the chuck wagon and get some of the boys to get the hoodlum wagon ready. Just leave three men here at the house to keep an eye on things. By dawn we can be high in the hills and ready to start a gather."

Gorevin shrugged, then stalked out to the yard, his shrill yell carrying clearly through the night.

"Roll out, everybody! We're ridin'!"

Long before dawn laid its pink and rose fan of brilliance across the heavens, the Falling S crew was a-saddle. Purple shadows lingered in the deep-walled canyons while on the higher crags that pierced the sky liquid fire ebbed and flowed.

All about them was a rugged, untamed land. Cattle that had freely roamed the thickets were hidden in treacherous ravines and dry washes. It would be a big job and a tiring one, but led by a grim and resolute Lee Standish, the Falling S punchers spread out to start their systematic search.

Spurring their horses into the tangled brakes, they flushed wild-eyed steers out into the open. They crashed recklessly through brush, clambered up slippery slopes, foundered in shifting sands.

No man worked harder than Lee Standish. He attacked the most treacherous gullies, his white stallion picking his way unerringly through the brush. Eyes slitted because of the glaring sun, sweat and dust mingling in a muddy, streaked pattern on his craggy face, he drove Whitey after the bawling, protesting strays.

Yet, in spite of his labor, by noon he had only succeeded in pushing fifteen critters down to the wide basin where a redheaded puncher held them in a crude rope and brush corral.

By the time dusk had fallen and the weary Falling S punchers threw themselves down at the cook fire they had accounted for only one hundred head in the gather.

Ben Fuller, a squat, gray-haired waddy past middle age with faded blue eyes set in a face that was burned and seared the color of saddle leather, grinned at the Falling S owner.

"I reckon we earned our chuck tonight."

"Yeah, and by the end of the week we'll be so dog-tired we won't even be able to eat," added redheaded Lynn Boyle with a grin.

Standish said nothing for the moment. These men were not complaining. They were just talking. Both Fuller and Boyle had been with the Falling S for a long time, and he knew he could not look for two more loyal hands.

Only Gorevin seemed moody and reflective. He'd pitched in and worked as hard as the rest of them. But looking at him, Standish sensed that the ramrod considered his boss' attempt to get a beef herd together, virtually hopeless. Yet, seeing that increased Standish's resolve all the more.

"We'll keep on workin' the draws and canyons, bearin' south toward the holdin' corral," he said slowly. "I won't be with yuh in the mornin'. Goin' to ride east along the line adjoinin' Buchan's Circle B to see how many critters we got grazin' up there. I'll be back in the afternoon to help with the gather."

Gorevin looked up at the announcement, a quickening interest showing in his eyes, but he made no comment.

Chapter Two

The next morning, after Gorevin and the crew had left camp to continue their beef roundup, Standish saddled Whitey. The animal was a rangy stallion with arched neck and noble, upthrust head. Nearly sixteen hands high, an alert wildness stirring the deep chest and trim barrel, the stallion suggested speed and endurance.

Resting one firm hand back of the horn, Standish hoisted his supple body into the saddle and turned east toward the Circle B.

Fifteen minutes later he entered a long, troughlike valley floored with lush green grass and broken by a timber-crowned ridge that sliced across its eastern tip. At the valley's end he took a steep side trail which rambled over the spine of the adjoining ridge.

After a mile of steady going the trees thinned out and became a wide upland meadow. Then in the distance he saw the cedar posts and wire strands of his line fence.

The sound of hoofs coming down the slope opposite him made Standish stiffen in the saddle, his hand instinctively sliding back toward his holstered gun. As the other horsemen came nearer Standish recognized the features of Jess Hawley, the government weather expert who was staying with Adam Brill. Standish drew up and waited for Hawley to approach.

"Howdy," greeted the weather man.

Standish nodded, not saying anything for the moment while he studied the other man.

Hawley was an extremely thin man with a face that

looked as if it had been pinched by a long siege of hunger. His eyes were black under sparse brows. There was a furtive restlessness in their dark, unfriendly depths.

"What are yuh doin' on Fallin' S range?" Standish asked.

Hawley shifted a trifle uneasily in the saddle.

"Just gatherin' some weather data," he answered.

"Yore work shore brings yuh out early," observed Standish noting Hawley's uneasiness and eagerness to get away.

"Yeah—yeah, it does," Hawley agreed quickly. He lifted the reins and his horse walked on past Standish. "Well, I've got to be ridin' into town," he added hastily.

Standish let him go, then pushed on along the line fence across land that now turned steadily rougher. He was surprised and a little worried that he had not spotted any Falling S steers. He should have had occasional glimpses of part of the small herd of yearlings left to graze this portion of the range, yet the hills and slopes were strangely empty.

Suddenly he came to a wide break in the line fence and he pulled up at once, dismounting to regard a confusing welter of cattle tracks that led back and forth between Falling S and Circle B land.

A premonition of trouble struck him when he noted that the break in the fence was a clean one, evidently done with wire cutters, and that most of the tracks led away from the Circle B onto his own land. In addition, another set of prints meandered from the Falling S onto Circle B range.

It was this odd circumstance coupled with the disappearance of the Falling S yearlings that impelled Standish to remount and push Whitey through the gap.

He followed the plainly marked trail for two miles across Buchan's property, his uneasiness constantly growing. At last, he topped a wooded slope. From this point he could look down upon a grassy bowl. White speckled blurs dotted the clearing close to the hazy shimmer of a Circle B waterhole.

Peering intently at the scene, Standish waited for the pattern to ebb and flow. But the scene remained immobile, and immediately a bell of warning rang in his brain and he knew why those cattle weren't moving. They couldn't move because they were dead!

Lips settling in a solid wedge across his bronzed face, Standish spurred Whitey down the incline. The stallion went buck-jumping past scattered brush clumps to the bottom of the grade.

Three sides of the clearing were lined by chaparral, and the grassy glade which surrounded the waterhole itself was littered with more than a score of steers. A nauseous feeling struck the pit of his stomach when he noted their swollen, bloated bodies. All of the critters had been dead for some time, but even the searing heat of the sun could not have accounted for their bloated appearance.

"Somethin' wrong here, Whitey," Standish murmured to the stallion, emptying his sinewy body from the hull. "Them critters don't look natural. Reckon I'll have a look around."

Standish's words were gentle and unruffled, but bunched muscles were riding his strong jawline, hinting at anger lightly held in leash.

High-heeling his way among the swollen carcasses, Standish saw with a shocked surprise that most of the cattle were Falling S yearlings. This was his answer to the strange disappearance of the small herd of young beef. But here and there, scattered among the other bodies, sprawled an occasional Circle B steer.

Near several stiffened shapes he saw a large block of salt, its surface gleaming with loose, shining crystals. Eyes narrowing dangerously, he picked it up and examined it closely.

"A poisoned salt lick!" he murmured.

He cursed softly, wondering who had placed it there and whose cattle it was meant to kill and why. And just what connection did it have with that cut line fence and the unmistakable signs of a large herd of cattle having moved from Buchan's range to the Falling S?

He wasn't surprised at finding the poisoned salt block —the sight of those bloated bodies pointed immediately to poison and what easier way to accomplish the death of cattle than through poisoned salt or water?

A crackling sound in the brush behind him and the creak of saddle leather whirled Standish around, pulling him to his feet.

"Reach for the sky, Standish!" shrilled a harsh, compelling voice.

Lee Standish cursed soundlessly as three horsemen spurred out of the chaparral. Three leveled six-guns menaced him, and the faces of the men behind those guns were utterly hard. Slowly Standish dropped the salt block, his hands lifting shoulder high.

"Kip Randall!" he blurted, speaking the words as if they left a bad taste in his mouth.

"The same," murmured Kip Randall, foreman of the Circle B. "We've got yuh dead to rights, I reckon. Those are poisoned cattle if I ever saw any and I reckon yuh're the jigger responsible."

The Circle B ramrod was a heavy-featured man, brawny and powerful in build. His lips were thick and fleshy, and his broad nose had been punched flat. He had raven-black hair that grew close to a narrow, sloping forehead.

Dark, shaggy brows served as a hood for his needle-point black eyes. Twin cartridge belts, sagging under the weight of menacing forty-fives draped his middle. There was a rough, untamed look about him and the two punchers, Ed Petrie and Jim Fargo, had the same tough, unyielding cast in their features.

"Kip, it shore looks like Buchan was right when he said Standish might be the jasper behind the rustlin'," grunted Fargo, a narrow-jawed man with a stubble of beard on his pear-shaped swarthy face.

A hard deadliness spread outward from the corners of Lee Standish's long mouth. He stood there, wide-legged, facing these men and coldly gauging his chances of making a break. Slowly, then, discretion crowded the rashness out of his brain. He didn't have a chance. Before he could dig for his gun his body would be tunneled by slugs.

"Mebbe you know how this salt block got here, Randall," he murmured, the meaning of his statement very clear.

Randall laughed harshly and a stinging malice entered his eyes.

"Yeah. You put it there, my friend. That poisoned salt block is proof enough for me that yuh're tryin' to smash Brad Buchan by killin' off his cattle."

"Yuh're crazy, Randall," snapped Standish, his eyes hard and bright. "I found a break in my line fence and saw where a lot of cattle had moved back and forth between the Falling S and the Circle B. I back-tracked here and found this poisoned beef." He paused for a moment and his voice fell, but a note of harsher insistence crept into it. "If yuh'll look past yore nose yuh'll see that most of the critters are Fallin' S yearlings. Would I be fool enough to kill my own cattle?"

"No," replied Randall, making an arrogant, domineering shape in the saddle, "but yuh wouldn't mind losin' some of yore own cows if yuh could kill enough Circle B beef to back Buchan to the wall. Or, mebbe yuh were just plumb careless when yuh cut that fence, forgettin' that the water would attract the critters grazin' yore north pasture."

"Why, you low-down—" began Standish, temper storming up through his veins in a hot, flaming tide.

"Don't try anythin' unless yuh want hot lead in yore belly!" warned Randall curtly as Standish's right hand dropped suddenly from shoulder level. "I wouldn't need much of an excuse to drill yuh." Standish glared at him. Then Randall, his eyes never leaving Standish, spoke to Fargo. "Take his hogleg and watch out for tricks."

Standish was trembling with rage when Jim Fargo dismounted and came toward him, but he made no further move of resistance, and permitted his holster to be emptied.

Arms coming down to his sides, fists knotting into hard, knuckled spheres, Standish looked directly at the Circle B foreman.

"You seem mighty anxious to pin everythin' on the Falling S," he murmured. "So blasted anxious, in fact, that I figger the whole thing is a frame-up engineered by you or yore boss."

Randall walked his horse up to Standish. The Circle B foreman smiled, but there was malice and hate in the gesture. It made Standish wary, yet he wasn't quite prepared when Randall leaned swiftly out of his saddle and slugged Standish alongside of the head with a downchopping gun barrel.

Standish reeled dizzily, almost pitching to his knees. Only his high-crowned sombrero kept him from being knocked out. As it was, his head began to throb with pain and he stared at Randall out of eyes misted over with the crimson haze of fury.

"That's somethin' I'll owe yuh, Randall, and pay yuh back with interest," he stated thinly.

Fargo and Petrie laughed in humorless fashion.

"Yuh'll never get the chance." The Circle B foreman's eyes bored into Standish. "It wasn't just luck that brought us to this waterhole. An hour or two before dawn this mornin' a band of hooded raiders ran off a herd of Circle

B beef. They left a trail and we were followin' it when we found you here. The trail seems to head straight for the Falling S which probably explains the gap in yore line fence. I reckon we'll take yuh along while we trail that beef. And remember, if yuh make one break yuh'll stop a bellyful of lead."

His shoulders stiffly erect, Lee Standish went to Whitey and lifted himself into the saddle. There was an ache in his skull where the gun barrel had struck. But even through that dull pain, the shadow of violence to come filtered into his mind.

He knew now from the veiled threat in Randall's words, from the wicked scrutiny of Randall's two companions that he was starting out on a one-way trip to doom. And the more he thought about it, the greater his anger became and the more he wondered whether Randall's appearance was accidental or pre-arranged.

At the moment the vague suspicion entered his mind that Buchan, toward whom he had always felt a natural antagonism, might have ordered this raid on his own beef to brand him as a rustler.

"All right, let's move," growled Randall. "I'll ride ahead. Fargo, you and Petrie take up the rear and keep yore cutters fisted."

Standish said nothing and turned Whitey up the slope behind Randall's big bay gelding. Topping the ridge, they continued straight on for two miles until they reached the gap in the line fence and proceeded across Falling S range. The ground became cut by gullies and ravines and sandy washes, but still the sign was plain for everyone to read.

"Kip, the critters must be right ahead of us! I just heard one of them bawlin'!" yelled Fargo.

Standish scowled. Randall lifted his horse into a lope and drifted into a narrow, high-walled pass. They followed the winding trail for two hundred yards, then came out on a wide, grassy bowl almost completely rimmed by brush.

At the far end of the bowl the canyon widened and fell away into low, slanting, timbered ridges. Crashing through the chaparral, Randall and the others could see a small herd of cattle milling in front of them.

"Here they are!" snapped Randall. "And every critter is carryin' the Circle B brand!" He turned to face Standish and his eyes were like two glittering black marbles. "This is all the evidence we'll need to prove the Falling S is stealin' cattle. What do yuh say now?"

"That the whole business is a frame-up!" responded Standish bitterly. "That trail of stolen cattle was too blasted easy to follow—so easy, in fact, that it's mighty plain the gents who did the job wanted anyone that followed the sign to think the Falling S was guilty."

"And the Falling S is guilty!" roared Randall.

"That's the way you want it to appear," retorted Standish, his flaming eyes plucking at the Circle B foreman with a relentless intensity. "The more I think of it, the more I'm convinced this whole thing was a sandy planned by Buchan as a cover-up."

"A cover-up for what?" snarled Randall.

"A cover-up for his own night-raidin'." Standish was all fire and brimstone now. "I'm bettin' you jiggers have been doin' the raidin' we're yellin' about. You cut my line fence, planted that salt lick, then drove them here, leavin' a plain trail!"

Randall's dark features turned heavier and more morose. He drew out his rope. Standish saw his intentions and plunged his spurs into Whitey. The gallant stallion plunged toward Randall. Standish rose in the saddle ready to launch himself at the Circle B foreman. But Fargo gigged his mount into Whitey, throwing the stallion off balance.

Once again a gun barrel stuck through Standish's sombrero and pain punished his skull in steady, throbbing sensations. He sagged, fighting the dark tide of oblivion with a powerful determination.

Quickly, while harsh amusement boiled in his throat, Randall built a loop and flocked it over Standish's bowed head. Standish jerked upright, his hands leaping to tear at the hemp. But Randall hauled the noose tight. The cord tore at Standish's throat and blood began to pump sickeningly into his head.

Fargo came up to bind the Falling S owner's hands behind his back with pigging string. Then with the rope very taut and the free end dabbed to Randall's horn, the latter thrust his face close to Standish.

"I reckon yuh know how people hate cattle thieves so we'll save the county the cost of puttin' up a gallows. The nearest cottonwood will do the trick."

Randall broke off to leer at Standish with a malicious triumph shining in his heavy-lidded eyes. Petrie approached and slapped Whitey's rump and the party went gigging up a low slope to a tree-covered knoll. Pausing beneath a cottonwood, Randall flung the rope end over the lowest branch, then wound it around his saddle horn again.

Standish's neck muscles were corded from the pressure of the noose around his gullet. Blood flushed his cheeks. A thick vein pulsed along the edge of his temple.

"How does it feel to know yuh're about to die?" taunted Randall.

"If yuh're expectin' me to crawl, beggin' for favors yuh can go plumb to blazes," Standish said hoarsely.

A shadow fell across his face. There was a frigid hollow in his chest and death was a cold wind blowing against him, but his eyes remained hard and defiant.

Lee Standish wasn't afraid of dying. It was going out like this without a chance to defend himself that filled him with a haunting bitterness. He would gladly have taken his chances against all three in gunsmoke, just so he met death fighting.

But they had him trapped. Their narrowed eyes held no mercy for him and in just a second Randall would give a signal. Then Petrie or Fargo would slap Whitey into motion and he, Standish, would be jerked from the hull to be left dangling at the end of a rope.

Breathing quickened in Standish's chest, but there was no cringe in him. He showed them a cold smile and a steely indifference that was as solid and unshakable as a brick wall.

"Let's get this over with," growled Petrie, somehow disturbed by the dark, unblinking directness of Standish's eyes.

"All right," snapped Randall. "Give his horse a belt."

Petrie nodded and clucked to his horse. He swept off his hat.

"Up with yore hands, everybody!" came a brisk command from the brush behind them.

Petrie whirled and cursed.

"It's that nester girl!" he yelled and shoved his mount forward.

A rifle barked and the sombrero flew out of Petrie's hand. He yelped in pain and jerked a reddening hand toward his side.

"Hold it! I can shoot better if I have to!" said the girl who stalked out of the chaparral, a smoking Winchester in her slender hands.

Randall started to swing up his Colt, then thought better of it when the long rifle barrel slid around to cover his chest.

"Stay outa this, gal!" raged Randall, his eyes sultry with anger.

There was an instant's strained silence broken only by the ominous snap of a spent shell being levered from the

Winchester. Standish craned his head around and his heart did a somersault beneath his ribs.

"Sally!"

The girl moved further out of the brush. For a moment, her eyes lingering on Standish were bright with warmth, then her attention shifted to the Circle B men and her chin lifted in strong resolve.

"Drop your guns!" she directed them.

"Sally," breathed Standish, a feeling of relief that was like a sweet pain, flooding through his muscles, "another second later and I'd have cashed my chips for good."

She said nothing for the moment, keeping the rifle trained on Randall's chest. There was something in the frenzied gleam of her eyes that warned Randall she was ready to shoot. The knowledge put a gray tinge to his cheeks and made him drop his twin Colts to the ground. Fargo and Petrie followed suit.

Sally Rockett was a shapely, beautiful girl with a softly rounded chin and a straight, swinging body. Autumn's light wind had whipped rosy tints in the smooth surface of her cheeks, while sunlight made its bright, clear flash against her blue eyes.

"By Godfrey, this proves yore tie-up with the nesters," said Jim Fargo. "Even a nester gal has to save yore gullet."

"Shut up," said the girl evenly. "I want one of you men to untie Lee's hands and take that noose off his neck. Quickly!"

Chapter Three

Grumbling curses, Fargo moved his horse close to Whitey. He produced a knife and slashed at Standish's bonds, freeing him, and then slipped the noose off his head.

Petrie, meanwhile, pretended a keen interest in stemming the flow of blood from his bullet-scoured hand, started to edge his horse behind Randall.

"Keep yore horse still," warned Standish gruffly, rubbing his wrists to restore circulation.

Petrie scowled, but stopped when he saw the dangerous look in Standish's face. The latter got down from Whitey, picked up his ivory-handled Colt which Fargo had thrown in the dust and thrust it in his holster. Then he remounted and risked a glance at the girl.

"Thanks, Sally," he murmured hoarsely, for some reason having difficulty bringing out the words. "I—I won't forget it."

"I won't forget it, either!" snapped Randall, his lips flattening against yellowed teeth.

The Circle B foreman glared at the girl before he went on.

"Sheriff Syl Manders will be glad to learn that yuh're aidin' a law-breaker. Me and the boys just caught Standish poisonin' some cattle at one of our waterholes. And yonder is a herd of Circle B beef rustled from our range by the Falling S."

Randall gestured toward the open basin. The girl turned to follow his gaze. For a moment an expression of shocked surprise crossed her features. Then she turned her attention back to Standish, and his unwavering glance was all the answer she needed.

"I don't believe it," she said stoutly.

Suddenly Sally uttered an involuntary cry, and she made a frantic and belated attempt to throw the Winchester up to her shoulder. Petrie, who had leaned over in his saddle, fumbling with his right boot, straightened up with a short-barreled hideout gun in his fist.

Ruddy flame clipped from the round, black bore. But even as that gun crashed, Standish prodded Whitey with his spurs, sending the animal lunging forward. At the same moment his .45 roared savagely.

Petrie yelped in agony and pitched drunkenly from the hull. Standish had aimed for the Circle B puncher's gun-hand, but the latter's horse had been moving while Standish shot and the bullet intended for his hand had entered his body a little below the left breast.

One glance at the lifeless huddle Petrie made in the dust told all of them the man was dead.

"I reckon it's time for yuh to clear out, Randall," murmured Standish tonelessly.

Kip Randall's eyes turned altogether black, and hate was a slow poison eating away at his restraint.

"Yuh've killed him!" he raged.

"He asked for it," Standish reminded him, regretting this killing more than he cared to admit. "Better load him on his horse and take him home." His voice dropped another notch, temper riding him hard. "Tell Buchan that the next time he tries to pull a rustlin' frame-up on me, he'd better be a little more clever about it."

"This killin' is yore finish," predicted Randall. "When Brad hears of this he'll swear out a warrant against yuh for murder and rustlin'."

"Vamose!" intoned Standish hotly. "I've got Sally here as a witness that Petrie drew first. But if it's trouble

Buchan wants, remind him that I aim to swear out a warrant myself against him for poisoning Falling S cattle and trying to frame a rustlin' charge on me."

Randall sneered, his glance bitter and deadly.

"This is cow country, my friend. How far do yuh think yuh'll get in defense against a murder charge with a nester for yore only witness? I aim to see yuh hanged before another day is gone!"

Cursing savagely, then, Randall and Fargo dismounted, hoisted Petrie's corpse to the saddle of his waiting horse and lashed the limp body down with rope. Then the two Circle B hands remounted and rode off.

Standish and Sally watched them lope out of sight beyond the next ridge. Then they turned and looked at each other during a brief, electrifying interval. As always, Sally's nearness and the smiling warmth of her eyes were a compelling call in the sunlight.

Standish saw her sway toward him and her eyes were brighter than they had ever been. Suddenly, then, her head was against his shoulder and his arms were hungry and violent, encircling her slender waist.

Her mouth met his fervently while the fierce, sweet flavor of her upset his emotions and his lips lost all their gentleness.

At length, she pushed away, glancing up at him with a grave concern showing on her cheeks.

"Oh, Lee, I'm worried," she murmured.

"About what?" he demanded.

"The trouble that's come upon this range," Sally told him. "Randall meant what he said. He'll bring the sheriff. You'll be charged with murder and my word won't mean a thing."

Her words trailed off, but the hollow dread showing in her voice filled Standish with a vague uneasiness. For Sally was right about Randall. No cowman jury—if he were arrested for Petrie's murder—would put any stock in the word of a nester girl, especially when she was defending a man who had practically aligned himself against his neighbors in the controversy between cattlemen and sodbusters.

He had shot in self-defense, but with antagonism running high against him he wouldn't stand a chance. There was nothing he could do now to change things. But he resolved that if Buchan tried to have him arrested, he'd fight back even if it meant starting a private war between the Circle B and the Falling S.

"I don't figger Brad Buchan will have the nerve to swear out a warrant against me," he told Sally, trying to put a note of firm conviction in his tone. Briefly he told her all the events leading up to his timely rescue by her. "Whoever stole that Circle B beef made an awkward attempt to make it look like the Falling S was guilty."

Sally's lovely face tilted toward him in serious appeal.

"Promise me you'll be careful," she urged.

"I will, but first I've got to see you safely home."

"No, Lee. You'd better not. Besides, I'll be all right. It was just fortunate that I had gone for a ride, planning to stop at your ranch on the way home or I wouldn't have found you. Hearing cattle bawling, I rode into the basin to investigate. It was then I saw you. Realizing you were in difficulty I hid in the chaparral."

Standish's attention had fastened upon the girl's first words. Now a puzzled frown ridged his brow and he asked a blunt question.

"Why don't you want me to ride home with you?"

"Because there's been more trouble," she blurted. "Outlaws wearing black hoods raided our place and Jim Holland's. They trampled most of Holland's truck garden and burned Dad's hay. Dad was so angry he called a meeting of all the nesters. He wants to take action. Oh, Lee, I'm afraid there's going to be more fighting and bloodshed. Daddy and the others are blaming the ranchers."

"Yeah," grunted Standish, "and the ranchers are blaming the nesters for the trouble they've been having."

Although Sally continued to protest that Standish should not ride back to the nester basin with her, he was adamant. Finally, she agreed and walked off into the brush where she had tethered her horse.

When they reached the basin they found a number of flatbed wagons and horses in the Rockett yard. Men with sun-wizened faces and work-hardened hands stood about in tight knots, talking loudly and angrily.

At sight of Standish and Sally the murmurs grew to shouts.

"There's one of the skunks now!" yelled one man.

"It's Lee Standish, and he rides a white horse!" said another.

Pressure stiffened Standish's jawline, and his right hand fell to his six-gun as the nesters rushed forward.

"There's the man who helped burn yore hay, Rockett!" shrilled Ace Gordon, a dark-skinned man with pale eyes and a furtive manner.

Led by Gordon, the nesters pushed close to Standish. Gordon reached up for Whitey's bridle.

With one deft hand Standish shook out a loop in his rope and flipped it over Gordon's head. Gordon strove to elude it, but the noose settled around his neck. Standish hauled the rope tight, leaned over and clubbed the nester alongside the head with his six-gun. Gordon reeled dizzily against the stallion.

"Keep yore hands off Gordon!" growled ruddy-cheeked Mike Carew, a double-barreled shotgun swinging to cover the young rancher.

Standish stiffened, seeing how violence rose in the face of every man in this group.

"Fair enough, Carew," he gritted, "but tell yore friends to keep their distance."

Gordon, recovering his senses, started to lurch away, digging for a Colt, but Standish's lashing voice held him back.

"Stay where you are, Gordon! I've got my gun lined on you and I'm waitin' for yuh to explain what yuh meant by sayin' that I helped burn Rockett's hay."

"Carew, why don't yuh shoot?" yelled one of the nesters.

"Go ahead. Let 'er flame," said Standish, his voice cold and implacable. "Just remember, though, that when I go out I'll take Gordon with me. I can't miss at this range."

Lee Standish's muscles grew taut and he waited for one of the nesters to make a break. They hated him with their eyes and with their long, set lips, but he braced himself solidly against them, defying them and showing them a reckless hard care.

Now Jube Rockett, Sally's father, detached himself from the massed group of nesters, and came to Whitey's head.

Rockett was a man in the middle forties, clad in gray flannel shirt, faded jeans and scuffed, low-heeled boots. His nose was beaked and reddened by the sun, and his surly mouth drooped at the corners in a gesture of stubborn intolerance. In height and build he closely resembled Ace Gordon.

"Standish, yore bluff about not knowin' what Gordon meant just won't go," he snapped tartly, his lantern jaw crawling forward as he indicated the charred ruins of several haystacks. "A band of masked men raided my place last night and did that damage. They were led by an hombre riding a white horse—and yuh're the only gent in Drayton who owns a white horse.

"Not content with that, you and yore men hit Mike Carew's place, ruined his truck garden and killed most of his chickens. And one of the raiders tossed a brick through a window of my cabin with a note attached to it. It was unsigned, and said us nesters have three days to clear outa the basin or suffer the consequences. I'll wager you know plenty about that note."

Shock and surprise rolled through Lee Standish. For just a brief instant his gaze lifted above the sodbusters to seek out Sally's eyes. She caught the meaning of his look and spoke quickly.

"I was afraid to tell you about the horse, Lee," she said. "I knew you'd be angry and that it would make you want to come here all the more. Dad and all the others believe you're responsible for the raids. I knew that if you rode home with me there'd be trouble."

"Sally, stay outa this!" blared Rockett, swinging his hot, enraged glance upon the girl. "I told yuh I didn't want you to have anythin' to do with this Standish hombre. He and his cowmen neighbors hate us, and Standish here has taken it upon himself to drive us out so he can gobble up the extra land."

Anger and bitterness was building up inside of Standish at the thought that someone in this valley was taking elaborate pains to frame him as the leader of the dreaded masked riders!

One look at the nesters had convinced him that they were sincere in their accusations. They honestly believed what they said, and that meant to cowmen and nesters alike he was branded as an owlhooter, a man to be shot or hung to the nearest tree.

"Rockett," Standish said tersely, his lips settling in a solid line as the nesters crowded closer and Mike Carew raised his shotgun in a threatening gesture, "that raid on your place and Carew's was no work of the Falling S. Me and the boys were workin' a beef gather all day yesterday in the North Hills. Yuh can check on that with Gorevin or—"

"Naturally yore men would back you up," sneered Rockett.

"It's still the truth," snapped Standish. "As you say, up

to now I've been the only man with a white horse, but I'm guessin' that some jigger has brought a white horse to lead the raiders against you and make you believe it was me.

"This morning I found a gap in my line fence and some of my own beef and Circle B beef poisoned. On top of that some Circle B cattle were driven off and cached in a hidden basin on my range to make it look like I was ramroddin' a rustlin' outfit."

"Mebbe you are!" snarled Ace Gordon, his eyes dark and brutal.

There was tense silence in the room, then Sally stepped forward.

"Dad! Mr. Gordon!" pleaded Sally. "Lee is telling the truth." Quickly she told about her rescue of Standish. "Randall and his men were going to hang him."

"And he probably deserved it," growled Gordon defiantly.

"Sally, get in the house!" roared Rockett. "I don't want you buttin' in here." Then he turned back to Standish, his eyes flaring. "Yuh're a fool to admit to us that Buchan caught yuh with them cattle."

"I'm playin' it straight," insisted Standish. "The trail of them cattle was so plain that a baby could've told that the beef was meant to be found without any trouble, and that the Falling S should be blamed—just like yuh've gone and blamed me for yore trouble here because one of the raiders rode a white horse."

Standish paused for a moment, and something in the bleak cast of his craggy features held them still.

"I've seen trouble slowly developing between you nesters and the cowmen for some time," he resumed. "While you have been raided, so have we. We've had cattle butchered and stolen. Buchan and all the others are blaming you gents for their losses just as yuh're blamin' me now. But hasn't it occurred to yuh that some jigger—

cowman or nester—may be deliberately incitin' a war between us so that we kill each other off, leavin' him kingpin of the range?"

"Yuh've got somethin' there," said Rockett, a strong contempt darkening his features. "Somebody is incitin' a war and yuh're the one responsible."

"Rush him!" growled one of the sodbusters. "The only way to break that gang of raiders is to kill its leader and there he is!"

An ominous roar of approval greeted that remark. Standish set himself grimly and hauled back on the reins, forcing Whitey to retreat. At the same time he jerked the rope taut, dragging Gordon backwards. as the nesters slowly but inexorably converged upon him.

"Okay, Rockett, if that's the way yore friends want it," he murmured tonelessly. The threat of death lay oppressive in the windless air, but Standish remained steel-nerved and gray-faced. "A cowman for a nester. It's an even exchange."

Every man in the crowd caught the meaning behind his words, and Ace Gordon's shrill voice lifted in abject panic.

"For God's sake, Rockett, call them off!" he pleaded.

Rockett's hot glance flicked to Standish's features. There was no compromise there and the nester scowled in helpless rage.

"Hold up, everybody!" Rockett called. Then to Standish he said in crisp, deadly tones: "Get out and don't come back to this basin again. That goes for you and all the other cattlemen. From now on we're sleeping with our guns in our hands."

"Just as yuh say, Rockett," Standish murmured. "I reckon I'll play it safe and take Gordon with me to the edge of the brush just to be shore none of yore friends get the notion to do some back-shootin'."

Briefly he smiled at Sally Rockett whose eyes regarded

him with a grave and worried concern. Then the smile left his face and his features turned hard and impassive again.

He swung Whitey around and forced Gordon to trot along at the end of the rope beside the stallion. Grimly he turned his back upon the nesters, not sure whether one of them would shoot. All of his muscles ached with the gnawing strain of waiting for the shock of lead that never came.

Finally, at the edge of the chaparral he freed Gordon.

"Join yore friends, Gordon," he directed.

Gordon's fingers scrubbed at his throat while a bitter virulence seeped from his narrowed eyes.

"I'll get even with you, Standish, if it's the last thing I do!" he rasped. "Just remember that."

Standish gave him a hard, straight glance.

"When that time comes it *will* be the last thing you do," he murmured tonelessly, then whirled off into the brush.

He rode hard, not worried by the fear of any pursuit, but plagued by a confusion of thoughts that left him no peace. Once more it had been brought home to him with irrevocable force that he stood alone, braced against an entire range.

That raid upon Rockett and the warning note called to mind the indignation meeting held at Buchan's spread two nights before. The ranchers had resolved to take action against the sodbusters, give them due warning to clear out or suffer the consequences. Was that raid, then, the first step in a secret cowman plan to oust the basin squatters, using hoods to hide their identity?

Or, as Standish was beginning to suspect, did the raid go deeper than that? Was it all part of some renegade scheme to pit the cowmen and nesters in a bloody conflict that would destroy the range?

Whatever was the true case, someone was intent upon

accomplishing his ruin. That stolen Circle B herd had quite evidently been meant to bring to a head the suspicions already entertained by Buchan, Runyan, Noonan and the other cowmen, that he, Standish, was not to be trusted. More, it branded him as an owlhooter. And the raid on the nesters finished him in the eyes of the basin men.

Only emptiness and misery waited for Standish in this wild land that had been his home ever since he was a button. He was caught in a terrible undertow of sinister forces that sought to overwhelm him. From now on he was a marked man, a prey to the guns of cowmen and nesters alike.

And yet, because of the streak of unyielding steel in him; because he was born to be hard, to resist oppression, he would fight back as long as life ran its strong and vital tide within him.

Chapter Four

Instead of riding directly to the roundup camp in the North Hills, Standish decided to stop off at the main ranch to check with the three punchers he had left there and see if everything was all right.

It was dark when he arrived and swung down from Whitey whom he left saddled with reins dragging. Three punchers strolled out of the bunkhouse to greet him. Behind them came Ed Gorevin.

"What are you doin' here, Ed?" Standish demanded of his foreman, as the four men moved around to the veranda at the front of the house.

"I'm glad to see yuh, Lee," breathed Gorevin, a strange, fathomless glint in his eyes. "I was worried when yuh didn't return to camp, so I rode down to see if yuh'd stopped off here. Besides, we needed more horses."

Standish nodded, his cheeks stiff with weariness and concern.

"How's the gather comin'?"

"Slow," said Gorevin. "Don't look like we'll make it in time."

"We've got to make it, do you hear?" blazed Standish, anger gashing his feelings with cruel spurs.

Gorevin scowled, stung by Standish's words.

"The men are only human," he said tartly.

Standish was about to make a curt reply when the rataplan of hoofs coming along the road from town drilled across the gloom.

"Riders coming," grunted one of the punchers.

"And from the sound I'd say there were a dozen men," murmured Standish. "Keep yore hands on yore guns. This may be trouble."

Standish's eyes thinned with a fierce intensity. He waited in the shadows, his body in a low crouch, his single Colt fisted while a wave of uneasiness put a hard pressure along his nerves.

But if this were an attack, the men were very bold about it, for they kept coming at a fast pace, making no attempt to muffle their approach. The beat of hoofs became louder, swelled to a drumming roar. Then a dozen horsemen swept in out of the shadows, lamplight from a front room of the house bathing them in yellow brilliance.

Standish felt warning prickle the tiny hairs at the base of his neck when he saw Sheriff Syl Manders at the head of the group and flanked on either side by Brad Buchan and Kip Randall. Behind those three ranged nine other riders recruited from town. There was a gun in every man's hand and keen, alert purpose shining in every face.

"What do you want, Manders?" demanded Standish, stalking away from the gloom shrouding the base of the veranda.

At Standish's movement Gorevin and the other three Falling S waddies slid apart, guns jutting from their fists.

"I want you," said the lawman huskily.

Manders was a pot-bellied man with florid cheeks, slack lips covered by a yellow-gray ram's horn mustache and blue eyes that were weak and watery. He was a man held down by caution and a fear of losing his job by not playing up to the influential men who ruled the range.

"Better make up yore mind to surrender peaceably," warned Brad Buchan, shifting his bulky shape in the saddle. "Randall told me about our stolen beef, and I've sworn out a warrant for yore arrest—for rustlin' and for the murder of Petrie."

"Drop yore gun, Standish," growled the lawman in a

blustering manner. "That order goes for yore men. This is the law talking."

"Yeah, and there's lead in our guns to back up that order," growled Randall, dismounting.

He moved warily toward Standish, holding out his hand for the latter's .45. Standish remained immobile, his narrow-eyed glance bracketing the Circle B ramrod with a cheerless force. Finally he shrugged and relinquished the weapon.

He was suddenly grim and bitter, cursing his carelessness. Randall and Buchan had wasted no time in moving against him. And now he saw how both Circle B men were eager for some show of resistance. One wrong move on his part and posse guns would crash, hurling a hail of lead into his body and the bodies of the loyal Falling S men who were ready to side him.

Somehow Standish knew that he couldn't sacrifice the lives of his punchers by trying to buck the unequal odds which faced them. And that was why he relinquished his Colt to Randall.

"There's two sides to the question of Petrie and that Circle B cattle," he informed Manders.

"Petrie tried to pull a sneak and I had to shoot him in self-defense. As for the cattle, that steal was framed to make it look like Falling S work. Stick around till mornin', sheriff, and yuh can see what a plain trail was left—too plain to be on the level. Besides, me and the crew spent all night at our roundup camp, workin' on a beef gather for railhead."

Syl Manners snorted, his mustache bristling with scorn.

"That's what you say, but I don't believe it. This is murder we're concerned about so I'm takin' you to the calaboose. You can tell yore story to a jury."

"Shore, if he lives that long," added Randall.

Lee Standish's insides were knotting with tension and he saw how this thing would be. They'd take him to Drayton, throw him in jail. After that maybe he'd live long enough to stand trial. But more than likely he'd be gallows bait for a blood-hungry mob.

If Randall or Buchan wanted him out of the way badly enough they could set up drinks for the town at some bar. With enough talk about the fate a murderer deserved and with enough rotgut to inflame men's passions and fog their brains, it wouldn't be difficult to recruit a mob to storm the jail and take the law into their own hands.

The smell of evil grew definitely stronger, and Standish was suddenly gazing into a future that instinct told him would be brief and altogether dark.

But once more the iron in him, the headlong recklessness that would ever impel him to resistance colored all of his thoughts. A wintry light seeped into his eyes and his face turned tougher than it had ever been. It should have warned the sheriff, but he was blinded by this opportunity to flaunt his authority.

"Quit stallin', Standish," Manders stated. "We're takin' yuh into town with us."

One of the Falling S punchers glanced at Standish, his long arms hooked at the elbows.

"Just say the word, Lee," he murmured thinly.

Standish shook his head and saw how surprise etched the ranny's face, and how Ed Gorevin grew entirely still.

"I want no gunplay," said Standish. Then to Manders: "All right, I'll go along. But I'll have to stop in the house a minute to check some entries in my tally book."

Manders heaved a sigh of relief, then grunted his assent. But Buchan's eyes flickered in speculative suspicion.

"Randall, you and Manders go inside with him," he directed.

Although it was in the sheriff's place to give any such orders, he feared the big rancher and had no desire to cross him. Swinging out of the saddle, he joined Randall and followed Standish toward the house.

"Go ahead, Standish," gritted Randall, hate seeping out all around his talk. "I just hope yuh try somethin' to give me an excuse to drill yuh."

At the top of the porch steps, Standish turned and his eyes met those of the Circle B foreman with a heat that was disconcerting.

"I figger that's yore speed, Randall," he declared. "Shootin' an hombre in the back."

Randall swore violently and punched the muzzle of his Colt into Standish's back. Outside the rest of the posse waited tensely. No one else moved, but a hint of violence to come greased everyone's nerves.

Entering the lamplit front room, Lee Standish increased his pace to ease away from the pressure of Randall's forty-five barrel.

There was an oblong table filled with papers in the center of the room, and Standish strode to the right of it. Manders swung to the left, and Randall followed relentlessly behind the Falling S owner.

Standish reached the end of the table and leaped to his left, his thigh striking the polished mahogany edge solidly. It tipped over and Standish followed it with a further lunge of his body. Randall yelled and his six-gun roared.

A bullet tugged at the slack of Standish's shirt. He saw Manders buckle at the knees as the table struck him, then go stumbling to the floor, striving desperately to line out his gun for a shot. Then Standish wheeled back to Randall.

The Circle B ramrod fired again at pointblank range, but Standish was charging in low. Flying metal gouged a furrow in his shoulder, then he hit Randall's chest with his head, knocking him back against the wall. He got his two hands on Randall's gun-wrist and gave it a mighty wrench.

Randall cursed in pain, dropping the weapon. Moving swiftly, Standish clawed his own weapon out of the ramrod's waistband and clubbed him over the head with the barrel.

Outside men began to yell and boots thumped across the porch. Manders got up, his legs entangled in the leg of the table. He flung a wild shot at Standish. But Standish was lunging toward the back door. He turned and snapped a high shot at the lawman, driving him to cover.

At the same moment Buchan and part of the posse crashed through the front door, caught a glimpse of Standish's figure disappearing through the yonder portal and opened up with a fusillade of lead. Bullets slammed into the wall, knocking down a spray of plaster, but none found their mark.

Standish bolted through his office and on past the kitchen. In the shadows filling the back yard he raced to Whitey and hit the saddle in a flying leap. The stallion started like an arrow shot from a bow at the touch of Standish's spurs, and by the time Buchan and the others reached the door to rake the night with their wicked gunfire, he was plunging away into the brush.

The posse swept around the side of the ranchhouse and drummed off in pursuit. But there was no horse on the range that could match Whitey for speed or endurance, and now the gallant animal answered his master's call for a headlong sprint that would carry him out of danger.

Guns continued to thunder wildly, but no lead came near the Falling S rancher. He sent Whitey plunging up a steep ridge, heading straight for the badlands, where he hoped to lose the posse in the tangle of ravines and gullies.

At the end of twenty minutes he sent the stallion slithering up a shaley slope and behind a ledge of rock that was shielded by a tall screen of brush. There he dismounted to let Whitey blow while he waited to detect sounds of approaching hoofs.

A long time later he heard a faint shouting, then a few horsemen—proving that the posse had already lost his trail and had split up to comb the timber—thudded past below him.

After he was certain that his pursuers would not return, he led Whitey back into the timber, moved on until he came to a creek where he prepared to make camp.

Chapter Five

Letting Whitey drink at the creek, he uncinched the saddle and staked the stallion out to graze. Then he proceeded to tear off a section of his undershirt and bathed the shallow wound in his shoulder. The bullet had barely grazed the flesh and, while it pained him and was a little stiff, he didn't expect it to give him much trouble.

He made a crude bandage, then flung himself on the ground. Sleep was long in coming even though his body cried out for rest. It occurred to him, now, with a forlorn sense of despair that he was a man on the dodge.

Cowmen, nesters and the law sought his life. From now on peril would be his constant companion.

Running away from the posse was the one thing to clearly condemn himself in the eyes of everyone. Yet, he'd had no alternative. There had been no mercy for him in the eyes of Buchan or Randall or any of the other possemen. And so he'd had to run.

Hope died to a feeble flicker in his heart, and the threat of disaster was very real and very strong in him. Yet, it wasn't just his own ruin that loomed above him. The welfare of an entire range was at stake, and suddenly he couldn't banish from his mind the fear that while he ran the hills from pillar to post, an outcast from a lawless land, the men whose devilish cunning had engineered those raids on the nesters and cowmen would continue their unholy crusade to plunge the range into a bloody, destructive war.

Now, because he had never gone around any obstacle

that he could meet face to face, because the will to fight back was a very part of his turbulent, reckless nature, he resolved to make an attempt to smash the strange and mysterious forces working toward the valley's ruination.

In the morning Lee Standish saddled Whitey and drifted slowly back toward the foothills. He was fully aware of the risks he ran. Capture by a posse might mean a swift hanging without benefit of a jury. And he didn't need to remind himself how slim would be his chances of survival if he should run into any of the tough Circle B crew.

Near noon he paused on a high wooded ridge overlooking his own ranch, saw a tight knot of riders assembled in the yard and realized it was part of the posse still on the hunt for him.

Hunger was beginning to add its gnawing pangs to the dull throb of weariness in his body, but he resigned himself bleakly to the prospect of going without food until evening.

Several times during that long and endless day he saw riders clambering among the hills questing for him, but he managed to avoid detection.

Near dusk he found himself near the shallow creek which meandered through the basin and saw the figure of a man toiling with a pick along the shaley sides of a ragged outcropping of rock twenty yards back from the stream. Emerging from the brush, Standish recognized the man.

"Hello, Rockett!"

"Get away from here!" snapped Rockett hoarsely, dropping his pick and fumbling for his rifle leaning against the rocks.

"You won't need that," warned Standish, his gun flipping into his hand. "Diggin' for gold?"

"Yeah, and don't think yuh're gonna take it away from me like yuh're tryin' to grab my land."

"Cattle are my business—not gold," reminded Standish. "Besides, it's time you got it into yore head that I'm not after anything that belongs to you. But here's advice, if the claim is any good, yuh'd better record it."

Rockett bristled angrily, his chin lifting.

"I'll do nothin' of the kind. If I was to file a claim, I'd have a score of men infestin' the creek lookin' for gold and there ain't any more here. It's a freak vein. I've quested along this whole cliff and this vein is all there is."

"All the more reason to protect it," said Standish.

There was a crackling sound in the brush some distance behind the Falling S rancher. Then a rifle roared and a bullet sped past Standish's head, smashing into the bole of a tree.

Standish curveted Whitey straight toward that sound, lifting Whitey into a quick run while he blistered the brush with a volley from his Colt. Whoever the hidden ambusher was he didn't attempt a second shot. Instead, a loud crashing in the timber announced the man's headlong flight.

Flinging himself in wild pursuit, Standish emptied his gun, then hauled up after traversing several hundred yards when that crashing sound of the other horseman dwindled away, telling him it was useless to continue the chase.

When he returned to the creek, Rockett had gathered up his tools and gripped his rifle. The cliff face had been smoothed over to disguise the fact that someone had been working around it.

"If that was one of yore friends tryin' to backshoot me, yuh'd better tell him to improve his aim," Standish grated.

"Yuh're crazy!" stormed Rockett. "I set no killer on yore trail. Not that you don't deserve it, but I do my shootin' face to face." He paused while shock and rage darkened his cheeks. "I was in line with that bullet. It could have been one of yore cowmen friends, or even one of yore own crew paid to get rid of me so yuh could grab my gold."

Standish's eyes flamed dangerously.

"Mebbe yuh failed to notice that bullet came a heap closer to me than it did to you. A little closer and it would have torn my head off. Somebody has been tryin' to frame me. Because that didn't get results I'm marked for murder. But if you think someone is honin' for yore gold, yuh'd better keep yore rifle handy."

His face a hard, brittle mask, Lee Standish turned his back on Rockett and rode off into the timber. And while he rode he wondered with a growing sense of unease if that rifle shot had been meant for him or Rockett. He had enemies on all sides now and wherever he traveled he knew he could expect a bullet in the back.

Who was the ambusher? A nester? A cowman? A Circle B puncher or some paid renegade? And had the man planned merely to kill him, Standish? Or, did he know about Rockett's gold discovery and planned to destroy Rockett to get at the treasure, Standish's presence merely complicating his problem and impelling him to try for Standish first?

These were the questions which plagued Lee Standish, but his troubled, turbulent mind could find no answer to them at the moment.

Putting the basin behind him, Lee Standish headed straight toward the Falling S roundup camp. The full shadows of darkness were on the land when he halted on a low ridge and watched his punchers hunkered around the cook-fire, wolfing down their bait of beans and beef and biscuits and coffee. He counted the figures around the blaze to make certain no possemen were there, before putting Whitey down the slope.

Ed Gorevin, saddling up a roan bronc from the cavvy,

whirled around at the muffled slur of the stallion's hoofs on the hard ground.

"Who's that?" demanded the ramrod. He dodged behind the darker bulk of his horse, a stray gleam of firelight shunting off the barrel of his drawn gun.

"Hold it, Ed," said Standish tersely.

"Lee! Hello!" gasped the foreman. "You don't know how close yuh came to stoppin' a bullet." He paused, then added, "You shouldn't have come. Manders and his posse have been scourin' the hills for yuh."

"I know. I've kept one jump ahead of 'em all day. But right now I'm hungry enough to eat a saddle without havin' it cooked."

There was a shadowed look on Gorevin's taciturn cheeks, then he shrugged and followed Standish toward the fire. Punchers leaped up at sight of their boss and crowded around him.

The cook took one look at Standish, then raked the Dutch oven back over the flowing coals. Firelight gleamed on weary, sweat-grimed faces. That dancing ruby glow etched out fatigue hollows in Standish's own face, and it did something more. It toughened the stubborn set of his square jaw, showed them all a man who was done with laughing, a man in whom rebellion flamed wildly.

When the cook handed Standish a plate of steaming food he fell to eating with a relish. During all that time no one spoke. Every man there seemed to know that the Falling S owner had come to some grim decision—a decision that affected them and perhaps the entire range—and they were waiting for him to talk.

"Where were yuh bound, Ed, when I rode in?" Standish inquired, his eyes lifting speculatively to the tall, stiff-legged ramrod.

A quick gleam came into Gorevin's eyes, but it vanished at once.

"I've got an uneasy feelin' there may be trouble tonight," he said slowly. "Thought I'd ride around and keep an eye on things."

"Yeah, it'd be tough if them masked raiders decided to try to scatter that herd of beef we're holdin' down below in that brush corral," chimed in a dark-skinned puncher.

"Better not take any chances," said Standish. "If them critters are run off we're done and everyone of you jaspers will be out of a job."

"What will you do now, Lee?" queried Gorevin. "No matter where yuh go, yuh're slated for trouble and maybe death. Yuh can't keep runnin' the hills."

Standish threw down his empty tin plate and rose to his feet.

"I've stopped runnin'," he murmured fiercely. "I've had plenty of time to think and I'm more than ever convinced that Brad Buchan framed that stolen beef and poisoned salt block on me. In fact, he may be the jigger behind the masked raiders terrorizin' the nesters and the cowmen."

"Yuh're shore of that?" demanded Gorevin intensely, his eyes suddenly fever bright.

"Not shore, but I aim to find out," snapped Standish. "And the first step will be to prove who set that salt block."

"How do you aim to do that?"

"I don't know." A knot of muscle stirred at the corner of Standish's jaw. He dropped the subject abruptly. For reasons unknown even to himself he refrained from mentioning his encounter with Rockett and the mysterious attempt at ambushing. "I'll be ridin' now. But first, I'm leavin' Whitey here for a rest. I'll pick him up the first chance I get. In the meantime, keep the boys at the gather and double the guard."

Saloons were going full blast when Lee Standish halted the black gelding he'd taken from the cavvy at the edge of Drayton. Wind-scoured, unpainted frame buildings lined both sides of the dusty, rutted street. The more pretentious structures boasted wooden awnings which extended over the walks, providing an oblong patch of shade as feeble protection from the beat of the sun's rays during the daytime.

But now the only light was the yellow brilliance of lamplight, flushing out from the saloons, the Cowmen's Hotel, Jason's Livery and a few other scattered establishments.

Sitting tall and straight in the saddle, hidden by shadows, Lee Standish was interested in none of these things. He was in town for a definite purpose, and he meant to carry it through.

He'd been fortunate on the way in from the North Hills in not encountering any other riders, but he could not be sure how long his luck would hold. Wanted by the law for murder and cattle rustling, he would be fair game for any man's gun. That thought hardened his jaw, put a wild, raw glint back in his eyes.

It was a long chance he was taking. And even if his suspicions proved to be correct, he wasn't quite sure what he would do next. But that was something to be taken care of when he came to it. And so he spurred the black gently and angled toward the darkened rear streets.

Riding three long blocks he halted the black at the narrow exit of an alley and dropped lightly to the ground. Street noises reached him dimly—the clack of chips, the clink of glasses, the raucous laughter of drinkers at the various bars, and the tinny clangor of a piano.

Ahead of him loomed two buildings. On his right was the one-story adobe structure that served as combined sheriff's office and jail. On the other side of the alley was the frail wooden hay and feed barn owned and operated by Slim Kawlor.

Moving to the back entrance, Standish peered straight

through the cavernous structure, glancing at the hay and grain stacked along the walls, the oats piled in wide bins. A lantern swung in a rafter above the main street entrance. Beneath its sputtering glow, seated on a rickety chair whose back was tilted against the doorway, lounged Kawlor.

The slender, long-limbed hay and feed man dropped the chair back upon its two front legs and nearly pitched to the ground when Standish's low voice carried through the gloom to him.

"Kawlor! It's me—Lee Standish. I've got to see yuh!"

Kawlor ran a shaky hand through his thinning yellow-gray hair, then turned into the barn. Stumbling through the darkness, a firm hand grabbed him, pulled him behind several tethered bundles of hay.

"I came to ask you a question," blurted Standish.

"Lee, boy, you shouldn't be in town," protested the oldster. "Yuh'll be shot on sight. They're sayin' yuh stole a herd of Circle B beef and that yuh're ramroddin' those mysterious night-riders."

Lee Standish's breathing quickened.

"Do you believe that, Slim?" he asked.

"Of course not," came the quick, violent reply. "I knew yore Dad before you and there never was a straighter man. I reckon yuh've got his blood in yore veins."

"I knew I could count on yuh as a friend." Standish relaxed and his grip on the oldster's arm relented in pressure.

"What did yuh want to know, Lee?"

"Besides sellin' hay and feed, yuh're the only one who sells salt blocks in Drayton," said Standish. "I want yuh to remember, if yuh can, who bought salt blocks from yuh in the last few days."

Kawlor breathed heavily through his nose while he considered the younger man's request. Then he slapped his thighs.

"Four days ago one of the hill ranchers bought a block," he said, speaking carefully. "Very next day Randall came in and bought a couple, and so did Chad Runyan."

Standish growled, disappointment rolling in him.

"That makes three who could have done it."

"Yuh're tryin' to find out who set that poisoned salt lick?"

"Yeah," grunted Standish, straightening suddenly. "Wait here, Slim. I aim to pay a visit to Bob Reynolds at his little drug shop."

Before the hay and feed man could say anything more, Standish had wheeled away, moving off to the rear street. There, he took the precaution to lead the black gelding into the enclosure. Swiftly, then, he ran off through the darkness. He passed another intersection, cut up a narrow alley, pausing at a side door of a dimly lit shop beside the stage office.

A blond-haired young man of medium height with dark blue eyes and a firm jaw opened the door at Standish's furtive knock. At sight of the Falling S owner his face brightened, then became shadowed with fear.

"Lee! Yuh shore took a chance of raisin' the devil by comin' to town. Manders really aims to get yuh. Come inside."

Bob Reynolds led Standish into the small cubicle that served as a prescription room behind the larger front room for the use of his few customers. Standish glanced up at the few shelves with their rows of neatly labelled bottles, then switched his attention to Reynolds.

"Bob," he murmured, "I want yuh to tell me if anybody bought poison from yuh recently." At Reynolds' lifted eyebrows, Standish went on to explain his reasons for desiring the information. "If yuh can tell me that, it may lead me to the men who are tryin' to frame me for rustlin' and murder!"

Reynolds' face hardened in sympathy for Standish's predicament.

"I don't blame yuh for bein' upset," he said. "They've got yuh backed against the wall."

"Yeah. It's either stay on the dodge or get hanged."

"Kip Randall was in here three days ago," said Reynolds. "He asked for some potassium cyanide. I didn't want to sell it to him, at first. He said somethin' about wantin' it to kill some coyotes which had been preyin' on Circle B yearlings."

A brilliant lustre built up in Standish's gray eyes.

"That stuff is poison?" he asked.

"It's deadly."

"Now we're gettin' somewhere," Standish murmured, an electric feeling of frenzy washing across his broad chest. "Would yuh be willin' to swear before the sheriff that yuh sold the stuff to Randall?"

Bob Reynolds' head came up and he smiled.

"Shore thing," he stated firmly.

"Fine. Stay put, Bob," Standish urged eagerly. "I've got a chore to do. Give me about two hours, then make it yore business to be strollin' near the jail. When yuh see me, come a-runnin'."

Without another word, Standish whirled away to the door. It closed lightly after him, and then his boots drummed down the alley. In two minutes he was back in the hay and feed barn giving similar instructions to Kawlor after which he swung up on the black again and sped out of town.

Avoiding the beaten trail which led to the hill ranches, he struck across rough country, angling toward the Circle B. With the proof he had secured that Buchan and Randall were definitely implicated in the cattle poisoning, Standish had decided upon a dangerous move.

Outside the law himself, he had determined to attempt

to capture Buchan single-handed, have him thrown in jail, and swear out counter charges against him—even though he might have to buck the entire Circle B crew to do it.

A half hour's rapid travel brought him onto Buchan's range, but instead of angling directly toward the ranch-house, he cut east toward his own spread, and at the end of another four miles he reached the waterhole where so many Falling S yearlings had died.

Approaching it, he slowed the black to a walk and proceeded cautiously lest some Circle B hands be stationed in the area. But closer examination revealed the place empty of cattle as well as men.

The carcasses of the dead beef had been removed and in the pale glitter of moonlight, the shallow pool of water, fed from a spring, shimmered like a dark mirror.

Standish was thankful for the moonlight because it aided him in his search for the extra evidence which he felt he needed to clinch a case against Brad Buchan. Yet, for fifteen minutes while he left the black idly grazing and he quested through the brush, scanning every yard of ground with narrowed eyes, his search went unrewarded.

Finally he stumbled upon the object he sought. Sliding down a shaley slope, he lost his balance and fell into a dry wash. And in a side crevice, wedged in firmly and deeply enough so no grazing cattle could get at it he found a block of salt.

He pulled it out eagerly. Then, thrusting his hand into the niche he brought forth a pasteboard box filled with a powdery substance. A label pasted on the outside advertised that it was poison. This, then, was the poisoned salt block which had been tossed away so it would not kill any more beef and would not link the Circle B to the affair.

Swiftly Standish climbed the slope and returned to

the waterhole. He pouched the salt block and poison in his saddlebags and swung aboard the black, heading toward the Circle B ranch buildings farther west.

Halting beneath a grove of cottonwoods, his eyes registered all the details of the yard with a keen attention.

The bunkhouse was in darkness, but that did not necessarily signify it was unoccupied so his wariness remained with him. It occurred to him with a jolting clarity how nearly impossible it would be to steal Brad Buchan from his own ranch with a dozen or so slick gunhands ready to side the rancher. Yet, the risk had to be run.

Lamplight streaming from the windows of the front room told Standish that his quarry was still up. Noiselessly, then, he dropped from the black and stole across the yard. For a long, tense moment he was clearly etched in the moonlight before he flattened himself against the log wall of the bunkhouse and crept up to the open window.

Listening intently, he heard no sound. If there were men inside and they were asleep he would certainly have detected some indications of snoring or heavy breathing. But there was nothing, so he was obliged to conclude the Circle B hands were not present.

Standish stiffened at the implications of that. Did that mean the men were bent on some booger business? Were they, in reality, the hooded raiders whose reign of terror had upset the entire range? That thought increased the gravity already lining his craggy cheeks.

He raced lightly around the back of the house, coming up on the far side to flatten himself against an open window of the front room. He heard voices and he recognized them instantly as belonging to Brad Buchan and Kip Randall!

Venturing a rapid glance inside, he saw that Buchan and Randall were alone in the room and were talking animatedly. The ramrod's presence doubled the odds and increased the risk.

An odd feeling rippled a ragged track across Standish's senses before his iron will, his indomitable courage impelled him to action.

Chapter Six

Hands placed firmly on the sill of the open window, Standish levered himself through the aperture. He hit the floor on wide-planted boots at the exact instant that Buchan and Randall, their backs to him, whirled around in shocked amazement and fear.

"Standish!" blurted Brad Buchan, crouching, his hands plummeting for his Colts.

"The same," responded Standish dryly.

Starting his draw evenly with Buchan and Randall, Standish shaded them both in a movement that was a symmetry of smoothness and speed.

"Don't make me shoot," he warned tersely, his gun barrel lined upon them with a steadiness that was unnerving.

Randall's splayed fingers, hooked above his Colts, came away slowly. Blood darkened his cheeks, and his hate was a terrible thing to see. But the sheer power of Standish's hard implacability falling like a dark, stifling shadow upon the Circle B ramrod held him entirely still.

Buchan was like a wild animal straining at a leash, eager to throw himself upon Standish, yet held back by the menace of that level gun and the greater menace in Standish's bronzed, stiff-lipped face.

"You blasted renegade!" fumed Buchan, his voice booming like a clap of thunder in the room. "Yuh're wanted by the law for—"

"Shore, and you're wanted by me," cut in Standish. "And I've got yuh." The sound of Standish clicking back the hammer of his Colt scraped against the big man's nerves. "We'll be goin' for a little ride."

"Just what do you think yuh're gonna do?" asked Randall savagely.

Standish's gray eyes never left the faces of the two men.

"Why, I'm goin' to have yuh both tossed in jail for poisonin' Falling S beef," he stated. "I've got witnesses ready to testify that Randall bought some poison on the same day he bought a salt block."

"Yuh're crazy!" blurted Randall, but a faint hint of terror seemed to be chilling his features.

"Besides," went on Standish, "I've got the poisoned salt block and the poison in my saddlebags. I found it tonight about two hundred yards from the waterhole where my yearlings died."

"Yuh'll never get us to town," said Buchan, glowering darkly. "Just one yell from me will bring a flock of hands runnin' down here."

Standish's features remained grave and unsmiling. Hate and bitterness were a consistent torment festering in his heart.

"Go ahead and yell," he murmured. "I made shore the bunkhouse was empty before I came up to the house. So it's just the three of us." His voice dropped a notch, hard and challenging. "Mebbe I've got some ideas why yore gun-slick waddies are absent tonight."

"What do yuh mean by that?"

"Did yuh ever hear of the masked raiders that have been botherin' the nesters and the cowmen? Well—"

Standish deliberately let his words trail off, and his meaning was altogether clear to the Circle B owner.

Buchan's dark eyebrows drew down and he lunged forward, then stopped as he saw Standish's fingers whiten around his Colt.

"Don't try to pin that on me!" raged Buchan. "I figger you know more about that than anyone else in Drayton."

"I haven't time to argue the point with you now, so get moving toward the door," snapped Standish. "But first, I want you to drop yore belts and guns. Do it mighty careful like, too."

His face grim and resolute, Standish strode to the front door and took up his station there. He watched how Buchan's hands paused at his belt buckle, debating his chances of drawing iron. Randall, too, had his moment of doubt and hesitation. Then both men opened buckles and let their belts and guns clatter to the floor.

Randall moved forward, his eyes calculating and shrewd.

"You'll pay for this," he promised.

Standish said nothing. Randall strode past him, placed one boot on the veranda with Buchan lumbering heavily close behind him. For a brief moment Standish's attention left the foreman to center upon Buchan. And in that clock-tick of time Randall spun, lunging at Standish.

Leaping back swiftly, Standish chopped down with his gun barrel, heard the sodden "thock" of metal upon flesh and bone. Energy drained from Randall's big frame. He dropped, falling against Standish's legs and knocking him to the floor as Buchan hurled himself into the fray.

Buchan's massive body pinned Standish to the puncheons, and his hard-knuckled right fist smashed into the young rancher's face with an explosive power that made red lights dance in front of his eyes. Desperately Standish wrenched his body aside and he rammed the gun, which he had never relinquished, into Buchan's middle.

"This hogleg explodes in half a second unless yuh pile off," Standish warned, emphasizing his words with a jolting thrust of the weapon.

Buchan gasped in pain, then rolled clear. Standish climbed to his feet, considerably shaken up by the pounding he'd taken. Then Buchan rose, his brows dark, ominous thatches above his wickedly glaring eyes.

"Pick up yore ramrod and carry him out to the corral," Standish ordered the Circle B owner.

Randall lay inertly across the threshold of the front door. Grumbling in rage, Buchan picked him up and moved across the veranda and down the steps into the yard. Out at the corral Standish forced Buchan to rope and saddle two horses, then tie Randall into the saddle.

It was well after midnight when Lee Standish and his two captives entered Drayton by way of the darkened rear streets. All but one saloon had closed up for the night, and in front of this establishment three horses drowsed at the hitch-rack.

Reaching the main street by way of the alley which separated Kawlor's hay and feed barn from the jail, Standish leaped off his horse and rapped on the door of Sheriff Manders' office. Back of his office was a little anteroom fitted up with a cot where Manders usually slept.

A minute or two passed before they heard boots thumping along the floor of the office.

"Who is it?" demanded Manders' sleepy voice.

Standish risked a sweeping glance up and down the street and found the walks deserted. However, he caught a flicker of movement in the dark opening of the hay and feed barn and guessed that Kawlor was waiting. Yonder, down near the only saloon still open he thought he detected a man's shape limned in the lamplight. The man appeared to be looking toward the jail, then suddenly vanished into an alley.

Warning made its brittle stir in Standish, then, and he wondered if that man had been a Circle B puncher. If so, trouble could be expected almost at once. He heard Manders growl again and turned to Buchan, coming close to him with leveled gun.

"Sing out, Buchan," he grated. "Tell him yuh've got to see him about somethin' important!"

Buchan stared hotly at the Falling S owner.

"Open up, Manders!" he growled. "It's me—Buchan."

Standish slid around to Randall who had regained consciousness and with a knife slashed the rope that bound the foreman to the saddle.

"Get down—and fast!" he ordered in a terse whisper.

Standish heard the bolt slide back in the front door of the sheriff's office, then prodded Randall and Buchan up the steps as Manders swung the heavy door open.

"Buchan!" said Manders, his eyes bleared with sleep, a flickering lamp in his hands. He was incongruous in a long nightshirt over which he had slipped trousers and boots. Suddenly he saw Standish. "What are yuh—?"

He got no further because Standish gave Buchan a shove that sent him crashing into Randall, and the two Circle B men nearly knocked the lawman off his feet as Standish crowded in behind them, his gun fisted.

"Don't yell!" gritted Standish to the sheriff. "I've brought yuh two prisoners for yore jail!"

In the dim light of the lamp he saw Manders' yellow-gray mustache quiver with indignation.

"You can't do this," Manders protested. "Yuh're wanted for murder, so yuh're under arrest."

"Yuh're not arrestin' me," said Standish grimly. "Yuh're arrestin' these two polecats for poisonin' a herd of my yearlings. And while they're in jail I aim to round up some more proof that Buchan here had his own herd stolen and planted on my range to frame me."

A cold sweat oiled the sheriff's seamed features.

"Yuh're talkin' loco. Don't forget yuh killed Petrie."

"He had it comin', and I don't aim to die for skinnin' a skunk." Standish's voice was low and deadly. "Randall, Fargo and Petrie were fixin' to hang me on a framed charge of rustlin' and when Sally Rockett got the drop on 'em with her rifles, Petrie tried to pull a sneak."

"If that's so," argued the sheriff, looking oddly at Buchan and Randall, "you ought to be willin' to submit and await trial."

Lee Standish snorted in derisive bitterness.

"Manders, yuh've probably heard what went on at that cowmen's meeting at Buchan's spread t'other night, and mebbe yuh've heard how those masked raiders who struck at the nesters were led by a gent ridin' a white horse—another trick designed to frame me—so you ought to be able to figger how long I'd last in yore jail.

"No, friend Manders, I'm playin' this game the only way it can be played until I can get to the bottom of the deviltry plaguin' this range. Mebbe Buchan here is behind it. I aim to find out for shore."

Standish turned slightly as two men moved up to the half-open door. One glance showed him it was Bob Reynolds and Slim Kawlor.

"Yuh're just in time," Standish greeted them. To Slim he said: "Mebbe yuh'd better shove the horses into the alley just in case anybody happens along the street and gets curious."

Kawlor nodded and stepped outside. Then Standish gestured meaningly to the front window, and Bob Reynolds walked over and jerked down the blind. Nothing much could be done about the open barred window facing the alley since it had no blind.

"All right, Manders," said Standish uncompromisingly when Kawlor returned. "I'm preferrin' charges against Buchan and Randall. I accuse them of setting a poisoned salt lick at a Circle B waterhole, then cuttin' my fence and lettin' some of my yearlings drift through. Kawlor will testify he sold a salt block to Kip Randall two days before it happened. And Reynolds swears Randall bought some poison from him."

"That proof don't mean a thing," blustered Buchan.

"No?" Standish hit him with the full impact of his bleak gaze. "I think it'll mean plenty. And out in my saddlebags are the salt block and the rest of the poison Randall didn't use. Reynolds will identify that as the stuff he sold to Randall the other day."

Buchan swung his enraged attention toward Manders.

"What kind of lawman are yuh, Manders?" he fumed. "Don't let him bluff yuh. He probably bribed Reynolds and Kawlor to—"

"Lee is tellin' the truth and I reckon I'll back him up. That's all," blazed Reynolds.

Rash instinct stirred Standish's long lips and his voice reached toward Manders, flat and hostile and relentless.

"Get yore keys, Sheriff, and open one of them cells."

Manders jumped when Standish wiggled the gun in his fist. He went to a hook on the wall and dragged down a ring of keys. Moving toward the anteroom, Standish herded Buchan and Randall right behind the lawman.

In the long corridor beyond the anteroom Manders opened one of the cell doors. Swearing savagely, the two Circle B men strode inside. Standish slammed the door shut. Buchan whirled and came up against the grating, his big hands gripping the bars and shaking them while his eyes bored wickedly into Standish.

"How long do yuh think I'll stay here, friend?" he demanded. "Yore charges won't stick and I'll be out to trail yuh plumb to hell!" His voice was charged with a consuming wrath. "Yuh've made this play, but yuh'll never make it stick. The next time I see yuh, I'll kill yuh."

Buchan broke off a moment and his slitted gaze slid around to bracket Reynolds and Kawlor.

"As for you two, my advice is to clear outa Drayton," he said sibilantly, "or yuh'll find out what happens to gents who try to buck me."

Bob Reynolds returned his gaze unflinchingly.

"We'll wait and see," he murmured, and Kawlor nodded surlily.

Then Standish broke in, speaking to the sheriff.

"Manders, in the mornin' I'm ridin' over to New Benton to contact Judge Rawley. I intend to give him the same information I gave yuh so if yuh value yore position as a law officer keep Buchan and Randall locked up."

Manders' eyes rolled out a faint apprehension that he couldn't conceal, and he regarded the Falling S rancher with a reluctant respect.

Standish turned on his heel and walked back to the office.

"Thanks for yore help," he told Reynolds and Kawlor.

"Glad to do it, Lee," said Kawlor. "Somehow I don't put much faith in Manders. If the Circle B was to find out about this and come howlin' down here, I reckon Manders would let Buchan and Randall go pronto."

Standish nodded and slid out the front door, then broke into a running leap that carried him into the dust beside the walk. He'd seen a furtive shadow dart away toward the alley. Now as he rounded the walk he heard the swift patter of boots, the whicker of a horse as the hidden man fled into the gloom.

Standish plunged down the alley. But the other man's passage had aroused the horses, and Buchan's big black reared up on hind legs and plunged against Standish. He was thrown, gasping, against the wall of the feed barn. By the time he regained his balance and worked his way past the milling animals the alley was empty and the sound of boots had dwindled away in the night.

He sprinted to the rear street, looked up and down, trying to pierce the gloom, but saw no sign of a running shape. His face settling grimly, he returned to the head of the alley where Reynolds and Kawlor were waiting.

"Who was it?" Reynolds asked.

"Don't know," Standish answered. "As I came out of

the office I saw the shadow of a man slinking away. He may have been listening."

For a moment he stood irresolute, then stepped back into the office. Manders was near the door and he jumped back, not sure what Standish had in mind.

"By the way," said Standish flatly, "don't try sending out a warning to the Circle B."

He didn't wait for an answer, but rejoined his companions in the street. Kawlor glanced skeptically at him and asked a blunt question.

"Where to now, Lee?"

"Out to the North Hills, I reckon, to grab some shuteye. Then in the mornin' I'll take Whitey and head for New Benton."

"I'm thinkin' yuh'd better not delay 'cause I've got a feelin' those two Circle B jaspers ain't gonna keep long in the calaboose."

Chapter Seven

Dawn was just two hours away when a band of riders trooped silently into the back streets of Drayton. With one exception every man rode a coal-black horse. The exception was a tall man who sat stiffly erect in the saddle of a milk-white stallion.

All wore black hoods that fell over their heads, covering their features down to the neck with two slits for eyeholes and another slit for the mouth. They came in silently, moving like dark wraiths, and pulled up behind Kawlor's hay and feed barn.

Dismounting, they came together in a tight knot while the rider of the white stallion barked short, crisp orders. Immediately the group split up. Three men slipped into the rear entrance of the hay and feed barn. Three more went running along the street, angling toward Bob Reynolds' drugstore, and the remaining four moved up the alley and hid in the shadows cloaking the front of the jail office.

The man who had ridden the white horse took several long, cylindrical objects out of his pocket and wedged them up against the door. He attached a length of fuse to them, scratched a match into flame and touched the leaping flare of light to the fuse.

Sputtering and shooting off bright yellow and red sparks, the fuse burned swiftly to the end, while the hooded men drew back a distance.

Abruptly the night's stillness was shattered by the booming roar of an explosion. The jail door splintered in a plume of dust and rising smoke. The four masked men shouldered through the wrecked portal, heads bent low. Charging into the anteroom, they collided with Sheriff Syl Manders jumping up from his cot.

"What happened?" he gasped, startled at the appearance of the hooded men.

"Surprise!" said the leader.

Without warning his right arm moved up, then down in a fast, down-chopping arc. Hard metal raked the lawman's skull and he collapsed.

"I've got the keys!" yelled one of the other men.

"All right," snapped the leader, fumbling at his black bandanna. "Open up the cell and get Buchan and Randall!"

Dimly they heard a shout from somewhere down the street. In a minute or two sleepy-eyed men and women would be stumbling out to see the cause of the explosion.

The leader followed his companions into the cellblock. A key grated in the lock and the door swung open.

"That blasted skunk, Standish!" fumed Randall, following Buchan into the corridor. "Wait till I get my hands on him."

"His hours are numbered," gritted Buchan.

"Let's get outa here," growled the leader. "That explosion will rouse the whole town. We'll take the sheriff with us."

Two of the hooded men picked up the lawman and carried him outside into the alley. Behind them raced Buchan, Randall and the leader of the renegades.

There was a sound of scuffling in the hay and feed barn, a muttered curse, then a cry of rage and pain. Buchan and Randall glanced questioningly at the masked man beside them, but he said nothing. In back of the feed barn the entire group paused near their saddled horses.

"Tell the boss I'm plumb thankful for rescuin' us,"

said Buchan to the tall leader. "How did he find out so quickly that we—"

"Never mind how we knew yuh were in the calaboose," snapped the renegade curtly. "We had our orders and carried 'em out. You, Buchan, are comin' with us to the hideout."

Buchan stiffened, alarm spreading to his cheeks.

"Something wrong?"

"I don't know," was the quick response. "It's the boss' orders. As for Randall, he's to ride back to the Circle B."

Windows were thrown open in the street and somebody's shrill yell cut into the gloom.

"Somethin's happened down at the jail!"

The hooded renegades leaped to their mounts. Twisting about in the saddle, the leader directed the two outlaws who carried Syl Manders to hoist him up in front of him. Then, after Randall had left for the Circle B, the renegade leader turned his mount and led the others off at a swift run in the opposite direction.

At the end of an hour's gruelling travel Buchan and his companions had circled deep into a land of tangled cliffs and steep, timber-shrouded trails.

Finally the hooded leader rode into a narrow-walled gulch. Following the defile for three hundred yards, he suddenly curveted his mount to the left and plunged straight into a thick patch of chaparral. Branches whipped and tore at their faces. After a moment, they emerged into a clearing, almost completely hemmed in by towering rock spires and clumps of brush.

In the very center of the glade sprawled a crude log cabin. Lamplight glimmered in the windows and the riders approached it boldly.

There was a long room running the length of the cabin with two sets of double-tiered bunks at either end. Along the far wall were a pair of doors, leading to smaller chambers out the back.

As Buchan crowded into the shack, closely followed by the two renegades carrying the unconscious sheriff, his wary glance slid directly to the bulky figure of a man seated at a table.

Like the rest of the owlhooters this man's features were entirely hidden by a black hood. Only his eyes gleamed hotly through the narrow slits in the dark cloth. Somehow, despite Buchan's own massive bulk, his arrogance, his love of power, he seemed to shrink and lose stature before this man's intent gaze.

"Pretty clumsy, Buchan, lettin' Standish capture you and Randall," the menacing figure at the table said in a gentle voice that was somehow all the more ominous for its mildness. "I thought yuh were gonna take care of him."

A bleak, brittle smile crossed Buchan's dark features.

"I intend to fix him for keeps the next time," he murmured, a brutal note in his talk. "He took us by surprise. That's all."

Now the tall, hooded figure who had led the raid on the jail swung toward the outlaw boss.

"What'll we do with Manders?"

"Toss him in the barn," snapped the other. "And see that there's always someone guarding him. He'll be better out of the way for the next week or so, until we have everything settled."

"Sorry I caused any trouble," said Buchan as the lawman was toted outside. "It won't happen again."

"If it does I'll be convinced I made a mistake in lettin' yuh in on this game," intoned the hooded man.

Buchan scowled. A hot reply came to his lips, but the fire in the other man's eyes made him drop his glance and ask a quiet question.

"How did yuh find out that me and Randall—"

"The details aren't important," was the mild, yet firm interruption. "I've got spies workin' for me where they mean the most."

The gentle voice paused and when it resumed, there was a rising irritation noticeable in it.

"That was a clumsy attempt you and Randall made to frame Standish. Yuh left too plain a trail with that stolen Circle B cattle yuh planted on his range, and yuh should have told Randall to buy the poison for the salt over in New Benton where he ain't known."

Buchan flushed in discomfort.

"Then yuh know about Kawlor and Reynolds, too?"

"Yeah. Their testimony combined with the evidence Standish found near the waterhole would have been enough to clap yuh behind bars for a spell if he got to Judge Hawley over in New Benton with the dope. It forced me to move against Kawlor and Reynolds."

The bulky hooded figure at the table stiffened, his long arm lifted in a gesture to command instant attention. "More riders comin' into the clearing. That should be the rest of the crew with Reynolds and Kawlor." He turned to one of the renegades who lounged in a corner. "Tell them to put Kawlor and Reynolds in the barn."

The man nodded and slid out the door.

"What'll yuh do with 'em?" Buchan inquired.

"I don't know," was the flat, disinterested reply. "The only way to keep them from spillin' what they knew was to bring 'em here. After we've got what we want in the valley, I'll decide what to do."

"But the main reason I called yuh here, Buchan, is that I want action pronto. Yuh promised to scare the sodbusters outa the valley and that yuh'd ruin Standish. So far yuh've done nothin'. The nesters are still here and they're gettin' bolder. I want them driven out."

Brad Buchan's tough, weather-hardened features turned heavier, more morose, and his eyes flickered angrily. "All I need to do is let him gather his herd, then scatter it."

The man in the black hood cursed softly.

"Leave Standish to me. Yore job is to get the nesters outa the basin. We've got to have all that basin land and the Fallin' S within ten days or the whole deal will fall through."

"Yuh'll get action," growled Buchan truculently. "But did yuh ever figger that the Circle B is doin' most of the dirty work and I still don't know what's behind it."

"Shore, yuh're doin' the dirty work," hissed the hooded man, "but yuh'll be cuttin' a juicy cake with me after it's all over."

"But why do you want all that land?"

"Yuh'll find out in due time. Take it from me it's bigger than yuh ever dreamed. And the fact that yuh don't know too much may keep yuh from gettin' ideas about pullin' a doublecross."

Buchan glowered, his shoulders stirring restlessly. Some of his natural arrogance flooded his cheeks and turned his voice unruly.

"What's to stop me from just movin' in on the nester basin and takin' it for myself or revealin' who you are?" he demanded.

"Plenty," snapped the hooded figure. "Did you forget that the federal authorities would be glad to learn that a certain Jack Roach, alias Brad Buchan, wanted for mail robbery and murder, can be found in Drayton?"

Buchan's features clouded with fury.

"How did yuh find out about that?" he raged.

"Never mind. It's enough that I know. If I hadn't called you in on this deal yuh wouldn't know a thing about it. Remember, the day you tell who I am will be your last on earth."

The hooded man at the desk paused, letting his words sink in, then gestured peremptorily toward the door.

"That's all, Buchan. Get busy with the nesters. And whenever you raid, have yore men wear the black hoods.

If there's any shooting, be shore not to leave any bodies for people to identify."

Buchan nodded surlily, turned toward the door and moved outside, passing the tall man who had engineered his rescue.

"Did yuh take care of Reynolds and Kawlor?" demanded the bulky boss of the renegades, looking at the tall man.

"Yeah. They're in the barn."

"Good!" The boss rubbed his hands together and his eyes held a strange, fathomless glitter. "Buchan's beginnin' to act up, and I don't trust him. We'll wait until he drives the nesters outa the basin, then we'll raid the Circle B."

"You aim to doublecross him, Boss?" the other man asked, his voice incredulous. "He's helped a lot with his men."

"Shore, but he's made a lot of mistakes." There was a brutal, calculating shrewdness in the bulky man's eyes and in his oily voice. "We've got enough men here to wipe him out. It'll mean less men to split the profits with after we get all the land. When this business is finished I'll be rich and the entire range will be in the palm of my hand."

He rose now and somehow the way he peered at the other men in the room, the shrewd and ruthless tone of his voice, the catlike way he walked, made him an ominous, disturbing figure.

"Wait here for me tomorrow night," he told the tall outlaw. "We'll put the finish on Standish, and I'm going along to see that there are no slips."

Chapter Eight

The sky was still dark but dawn was not far away when Lee Standish cantered into the Falling S roundup camp. Sleepy-eyed punchers rolled out of their blankets to greet him. He found Ed Gorevin walking away from the crude pole corral which held the remuda.

"Looks like I ain't the only one who's been ridin'," Standish observed, his eyes oddly intense as they switched from the ramrod's sweaty horse to his alkali-stained clothes. "You have trouble?"

"Some." Gorevin's voice was tight and so was his face. "I couldn't sleep so I rode around, looked in on Charlie Gumbert at the gather and circled through the hills. Some jiggers took a shot at me, then ran. I followed, but lost 'em."

"Got any idea who they were?" demanded Standish.

"No, but they may have wanted to scatter our beef."

Standish nodded, his features altogether grave.

"Lucky yuh got away. Better stop ridin' the hills alone at night."

"Take yore own advice, Lee," said Gorevin. "You've been takin' chances, too." His eyes, lifting to Standish's face, mirrored dark fleeting thoughts. "How did yuh make out?"

"Not bad," said Standish. "I took a chance and found Buchan and Randall alone at the Circle B. Got the drop on 'em, took them into town and forced Manders to throw them in the lock-up."

The other punchers crowding around in a tight circle

whistled in amazement, their eyes roundly admiring their young boss.

"How did yuh manage to do that, Lee?" demanded one ranny.

Briefly Standish explained, concluding with:

"I lined up Reynolds and Kawlor and they'll testify against Randall in regards to that salt block and the poison. On top o' that I've got the salt block and the remains of the poison in my saddlebags. I'll leave that evidence with Judge Hawley when I ride over to New Benton."

For a moment Ed Gorevin's features showed a mixture of conflicting emotions. Then a twisted smile wreathed his lips.

"Man, you did yoreself a piece of work," he acknowledged, "though yuh've still got to find out who's behind those raiders."

"That'll be my next move after I see Judge Hawley. In the meantime, Ed, keep the boys at the gather. I'll be back by dusk after I grab a few hours' shuteye here in camp. Yuh'd better stop by the ranch tomorrow evening to see how things are there, too."

The rannies talked among themselves for another ten minutes, then turned back to their blankets. To Lee Standish, worn out from a long day and night of being constantly on the move, sleep came almost instantly.

When he awoke the sun was beginning its swift climb above the serrated peaks and spires in the east. Gorevin and the crew had already ridden off, so after bolting down a light breakfast, Standish threw his rig on Whitey and headed for New Benton.

It was noon when he arrived in the railhead town, but he didn't pause to eat. He gave only the briefest of glances to the twin ribbons of steel gleaming under the hot sun, the long line of cattle chutes at the railroad siding.

Dismounting in front of the courthouse, he moved to

his saddlebags and explored inside with his hand. Then he halted and shocked dismay formed a cold lump in his stomach.

The salt block and the poison were gone! A mounting vibration of wrath beat up through his sinewy frame, and he cursed himself for not checking on their contents before leaving the roundup camp.

His bleak thoughts carried him back immediately to the scene in the Drayton jail when he'd surprised that furtive figure in the alley. Had that hidden man overheard all the talk in the jail? If so, he must have heard Standish mention where the salt block and poison were located, and had taken the stuff.

Either that, or someone in his own crew was working for the outlaws ravishing the district! Standish didn't like to consider that, but it might be true.

He blamed himself now for talking so openly among his punchers about his plans for making his charges against Buchan stick. There would have been ample time for one of the crew to steal the stuff out of his saddlebags while he slept.

The rising tide of his anger carried him headlong into Judge Hawley's chambers in the courthouse. Hawley, an old friend of Standish's father, listened attentively to his story, to his violent suspicions, his charges against Buchan and Randall, then shook his head.

Hawley was gray-haired, ruddy-cheeked with genial, good-natured features and a gentle, softly modulated voice.

"You're in a tough spot, Lee," he said gently. "Losing that salt block and poison definitely weakens your case, but I'll order Manders to transfer Buchan and Randall here for trial. If Reynolds and Kawlor stick to their stories we may get a conviction. It all depends. Yore evidence would clinch it. Buchan is a power in this country. Nobody likes to cross him.

"I'll do my best, but you'd better keep your eyes on Reynolds and Kawlor. See that nothing happens to them. And while you're at it, watch your step. Up here we've been hearing stories about you. I don't believe them—but others do, and it won't help your case. You may find yourself and Falling S on trial instead of the Circle B."

It was a long dismal ride home for Lee Standish. While Hawley had promised him all possible help, he had the dull conviction that it would not be enough. In Drayton he was a hunted man. And in New Benton public opinion was already building up against him, as evidenced in the taut, hostile scrutiny he'd been subjected to by the range-hardened men he'd passed in the streets. The news of the stolen Circle B herd and Petrie's killing had traveled rapidly and the judgment of these men was not kindly or sympathetic.

Reaching the Falling S roundup camp at dusk, he saw how Lynn Boyle and Ben Fuller hastened toward him, and instinctively knew that something had gone wrong.

"Yore case against Buchan and Randall has blown sky-high!" dour-faced Ben Fuller told him.

A steely glitter came into Standish's gray eyes. His hands were rough when they grabbed Fuller's shoulders. "So you know about that stolen evidence!"

"Stolen evidence!" echoed Fuller, his face frankly perplexed. "I don't know what—"

"I'm sorry, Ben," said Standish contritely. "For a minute I thought—never mind. What do you mean my case against the Circle B is washed up?"

"Just that," replied Fuller, his deep-set blue eyes grave and careworn. "One of Manders' deputies rode out from town late this morning with a fresh posse. Somebody blew up the front door of the jail last night and released Buchan and Randall. And Manders is gone! Not a sign of him anywhere!"

Standish's thoughts left an acid taste in his mouth.

"The Circle B—or the masked raiders—didn't lose any time," he growled tartly. "That means the hombre I surprised hangin' out in the alley while I was inside the jail with Buchan and the others overheard our talk. He must have run off and got the Circle B. And the same jigger must have stolen that salt block and the poison out of my saddlebags."

"You lost yore evidence?" queried Fuller.

Standish explained, his voice low and strained.

"Whoever rescued Buchan and Randall evidently took Manders to make shore he wouldn't do any talkin' either," he mused. "That means they're desperate and the stakes must be high. Manders don't amount to much, but he's the law. That just leaves me Reynolds and Kawlor, my two witnesses."

"I reckon yuh haven't even got Reynolds and Kawlor."

"What? Yuh mean—"

Fuller shrugged, his pale blue eyes matching the anger that was bannering from the steady, narrow-lidded eyes of Standish.

"Folks in town ain't seen any sign of Kawlor or Reynolds. Somebody said he heard a rumpus in the hay and feed barn about the time of the explosion. That's all. Nothing definite. I sent Lynn in to Drayton this afternoon and he brought back word that Reynolds' drugstore ain't been open all day."

"That makes it complete," ground out Standish savagely. "I'm right back where I started from. It's obvious Manders, Kawlor and Reynolds have been kidnapped so they couldn't talk. I've got to find 'em."

"Where'll yuh start to look?" inquired Boyle. "It's a cold trail."

Standish nodded, all the recklessness in him fully aroused now. His back was thoroughly to the wall and he moved in a deadly undertow of antagonism and hate.

He was about to answer Boyle when a puncher who had been stationed as a lookout on a high promontory above the camp came racing tward them, waving his arms and shouting.

"Lee! There's a fire over yonder to the west! Looks like it might be from the Falling S!"

A hollow feeling of dread twisted Standish's insides into a tight knot as he gazed in the direction the puncher indicated.

"Young is right!" howled Lynn Boyle. "It is a fire."

"Those blasted masked raiders!" gritted Ben Fuller.

A wicked rage pinched Lee Standish's features, and at this moment he was as dangerous as any man could be.

"Boyle, you stay here with the rest of the crew and watch the beef. I'll just take Ben and Dan Young with me. Come on, Ben."

Standish raced to the already weary Whitey and climbed aboard. Seldom did he ever use the spurs on the gallant stallion, but tonight he did, for a grim and terrible urgency rode his nerves.

He roared out of the camp with Fuller and Young lashing their mounts in a frantic attempt to keep pace with him. It was rough going over the treacherous terrain, but Standish kept Whitey at a dead run.

Somehow the horse picked his way unerringly across the rugged land while the miles flew by under foot. And all the while that leaping red glow in the sky grew in brilliance, and hope died to a faint flicker in Standish's breast.

They were within a mile of the ranch and the flames were fully visible above the screening trees when a body of horsemen swept around a bend in the trail.

Six-guns began their harsh yammering and bullets droned about the Falling S riders. Colts leaped into their hands, blared savagely, lashing ruddy counter lances of brilliance across the gloom.

Close beside him Standish heard Dan Young's howling cry of agony. Twisting about in the kak, he saw the puncher's mount pitch him out of the saddle. Hurled through space, his body was a limp and lifeless thing, and that sight turned Lee Standish completely berserk. Outnumbered three to one, the two Falling S men bolted recklessly along the trail straight into the face of the headlong charge of those other riders.

Muzzle light washed redly back and forth between the trees. To Standish it seemed that he was riding full tilt into a sheet of crawling flame. He grunted in satisfaction as his Colt kicked back against his wrist, roaring its own song of death.

One of the hooded men flung up his hands toward the sky, then pitched drunkenly into space. Another rider dropped his flaming gun and clutched at his middle. Fuller emptied an outlaw saddle, then doubled up, grabbing for the horn.

Suddenly Whitey stumbled into a concealed hole in the trail, careened half to his knees. Intent upon his firing, Standish lost his knee-grip and was hurled head-first over the stallion's head. Arms outflung, he struck the ground on his shoulders, rolled over and slammed his head against a ragged rock outcropping. For a brief moment he fought desperately to retain his hold on consciousness. But the pull of that dark tide of oblivion was too strong and it engulfed him. . . .

The solid jarring motion of a horse's tread jolted up through the nerves of Lee Standish's body to bring him back to complete awareness. His head, which had been sagging against his chest, lifted and his eyes peered through a sea of reddish pain at the boulder-studded trail rolling by, and the hooded riders who hemmed him in.

"Boss," said one of the outlaws, "Standish is comin' to."

"Good," grunted a spare, even voice at the head of the

cavalcade. "I wanted him to know what he faced before he died because we're at Eagle's Nest now."

Eyes gleaming behind dark, slitted cowls stared in wicked amusement at Lee Standish as he strained at the ropes imprisoning his wrists behind his back.

He remembered being thrown from Whitey and striking the ground. Everything had gone black, then. Looking around, he saw that he was the only prisoner of these renegades. Which meant that they'd gotten Fuller and Young. Young had died in the very first seconds of the brief six-gun skirmish, while Fuller had sagged forward in his saddle immediately before he, Standish, was unhorsed.

Yonder, several miles to the rear he could see the dull red glow of flames and knew with a sinking heart that it signified the destruction of his ranch. And now bitterness and rage tugged at his mind with the inexorable power of a suction pump.

The riders halted and a bulky, ominous figure in a coal-black hood and glittering eyes cantered up beside him.

"Come out from behind that hood, Buchan!" Standish stormed.

"Guess again, my friend," taunted the bulky leader.

A puzzled frown knitted three parallel furrows in the Falling S owner's forehead. That voice was gentle, passionless, yet deliberately muffled to prevent recognition. There was a faintly familiar ring to it, but he couldn't place it at the moment.

"Well, if yuh're not Buchan, yuh're probably workin' for him," snapped Standish. "He's been honin' to ruin me on this range, first with that poisoned salt lick, then the frame-up for cattle stealing, and now the fire at my ranch."

The hooded man laughed softly, wickedly.

"That fire helps, my friend, but it's not quite all." There was a calm and studied brutality in the renegade's precise speech. "There's still yore beef herd in the North Hills. Even with that wiped out and a whole range against you, I figger yuh might make trouble because yuh're a fighter. That's why I can't afford to take any more chances with yuh.

"Tonight you die right on yore own range. It'll be just a case of a strange disappearance and no one will ever find yore body."

No change of expression marred the gray and implacable mask of Lee Standish's irregular face, though he thoroughly understood that he'd reached the end of the trail.

His sharp glance slid past the raiders, showing him a narrow glade bathed in the serene and silvery brilliance of moonlight. Near at hand bulked the huge rock mass called Bald Eagle Peak. It was rough, treacherous land on his own range which he kept free of cattle.

Towering majestically above him were the sleek gray flanges of rock, wide and serrated, spreading out like the pinions of a bird paused for flight. Those wings tapered off into narrowing shoulders. And in the center loomed another shiny mass, bald and bare of vegetation, notched and beaked like the head of an eagle.

The bulky figure in the saddle facing Standish noticed the direction of his gaze and chuckled.

"I reckon yuh know this glade ends in an abrupt precipice," he said. "Fitfty yards below, Bald Eagle Creek spills outa the cliff. Once you land in there nobody but the fish will ever find yore body again—especially if it's weighted with a rock!"

Standish wrenched desperately at his bonds but they remained firm and unyielding. Ironically enough his initialed, ivory-handled Colt which he remembered dropping in his fall, had been replaced in his scabbard. That was evidence in itself that these outlaws never expected him to be able to use it again.

"I don't know who you are," said Standish thinly, "but anyone could notice yore skunk smell a mile off."

The hooded man laughed softly, then swung his knuckled fist to Standish's face. The blow stunned him, increased the pain in his skull already throbbing from the impact of his fall against the rock. Blood ran warmly in his mouth.

"Mister," he murmured defiantly, "all I'd like is ten minutes with yuh with my bare hands. I ain't scared of dying, but I shore would like to square accounts for all the trouble yuh've brought to the valley."

"It can't be avoided," said the bulky man flatly. "I aim to rule this range and you stand in my way."

The leader broke off and spoke to one of the other riders.

"All right. Tie that weight to his legs."

One of the renegades who had dismounted approached, carrying a huge rock around which a stout strand of rope had been securely anchored in a deep-lipped groove. The other end of the rope was now fastened to Standish's right ankle. It was a tremendous weight and almost dragged him out of the saddle. As it was he had to strain all his muscles to keep his balance.

Strangely enough he felt no fear, only a deep regret that he had failed. The renegades had proved too clever, too powerful. His efforts to combat them were about to terminate in death. Yet even that grim thought could not dim the spark of stubborn resistance still burning within him.

Fifty yards below Standish heard the wild, musical passage of the mountain stream as it gushed out of a notch in the bluff, seeping into the canyon head in crystal-laced, foaming cascades. At this moment it was a provocative, disturbing sound.

"Not a pleasant way to die, is it, Standish?" inquired the soft-voiced leader with a malice that was maddening.

Standish's eyes turned flinty and hard.

"I'll tell you about it when I come back to settle with you and yore friends," he gritted hoarsely.

There was an odd, compelling quality about that flat prediction that left the bulky outlaw leader unnerved. He remained mute and unmoving for dragging seconds of time before he blared a terse command.

"Over with him!"

Lee Standish's horizons closed down upon him. He took a deep breath while every nerve in his body throbbed and his lips were like a band of steel across his face.

He heard movement behind him, made a frantic attempt to knee Whitey into the left hand group of renegades. But somebody slugged him with a gun butt and he sagged lifelessly.

Then the outlaws were fanning Whitey toward the brink of disaster. The stallion skidded sharply, rearing on hind legs. A trumpeting animal scream rent the night, then horse and rider toppled into space.

The rock anchor lashed to his leg hauled Standish clear of Whitey at once, and he went plunging down and down into darkness. A sheet of water billowed into the air when his weighted body struck the brawling creek and torpedoed straight to the bottom.

Chapter Nine

Sally Rocket turned away from the stove and she crossed the front room of the rough-hewn cabin with a steaming pot of coffee in her hands. There were six men in the room including her father and to each of them she gave a mug of the hot coffee.

A stubborn, bleak purpose showed in Jube Rockett's lantern-jawed features while the rest of these men showed the sure signs of trouble and adversity and fear.

"Mebbe those outlaws were only bluffin'," said quiet-voiced Jim Holland. "We ain't heard from them since that last raid and warning. Besides, we've all got families to think of. Rather than stay to fight and get killed, I'll clear out."

"That's just what they're hopin' you do," snapped Mike Carew, his rawboned features flushing with temper. "Me, I'm tired of runnin'. Three times I've built a home and plowed up a quarter of land only to be driven out by range hogs."

Rockett nodded, but Jim Holland protested again and he was sided by Lear Graves, a timid man with a hollow, consumptive look.

"I agree with Mike Carew," said Rockett. He rose from his chair and paced up and down the room. "The only way to lick those cowmen—and yuh can bet yore last dollar they're the renegades—is to fight them at their own game. That's why I've hired Ira Stone there."

At the mention of that name all the nesters turned to regard the stony-faced man who lounged against a wall of the cabin. His features were altogether hard and expressionless, his lips thin to the point of severity and his eyes were cold, fathomless pits in his bronzed skin.

"He's a gunman," blurted Ace Gordon, his eyes blinking nervously.

"Shore he's a gunman," agreed Rockett surlily. "And I'm paying him gunman's wages—sixty a month and found."

"Where yuh gettin' the money to hire gunslicks?" demanded Gordon with a sneer. "Somebody leave you a fortune or did yuh rob a bank?"

Rockett's lips moved nervously and Gordon saw his eyes slide involuntarily to the center of the room where an oblong length of carpet covered the rough plank floor.

"I've got no fortune and I robbed no bank," snapped Rockett irritably. "I'm usin' money I've worked and slaved to save."

Gordon smiled, a speculative glint in his blinking eyes.

"Hiring gunmen is out of the question," said Mike Carew. "If yuh've got the money for it, yuh're luckier than the rest of us. I'm mighty glad to keep my family in food and clothing."

"Well, I'm goin' ahead," said Rockett. "But take my advice. If the rest of you can pool together to hire some more men like Ira here we could form a little army to smash back at Standish if he raids us again."

The door of the cabin smashed inward and four hooded men crowded into the room, six-guns fisted.

"It's too late for yore army, Rockett!" growled a tall man. "Yuh're movin' out tonight and we're here to see yuh do it."

Rockett stiffened, his eyes muddy with rage and futility. Ira Stone started to leap away from the open window at his back, hands plummeting to tied-down holsters, then halted. Slowly his hands lifted to his shoulders as a gun barrel poked at his back.

"That's better, mister!" said a sharp voice at the window.

Mike Carew was trembling with wrath. Ace Gordon's eyes were blinking, and Holland and Graves turned still with fear.

"You can't make us get out," growled Rockett.

"Shut up," said the dry, muffled voice of the tall, broad-shouldered leader of the raiders.

A man on his left turned his head.

"You want us to pile the furniture in the middle of the room and set it afire, Lee?" he asked.

The mention of that word "Lee" struck like a rifle shot into the room. Purple fury clouded Rockett's unyielding features, and Sally's face whitened until all the blood seemed to have drained out of her skin.

"I was right!" thundered Rockett. "Standish, you are the skunk that's tryin' to hog the range."

"You fool!" hissed the tall leader, his tones low and muffled, as he faced the outlaw who had spoken. "Watch yore tongue."

"Yuh dirty doublecrosser," breathed Mike Carew, "pretendin' to be our friends; tellin' us to unite and fight back, courtin' Sally here and all the while fixin' to stab us in the back."

"Lee!" cried Sally, a hurt bewilderment in her tone. She came half-blindly across the room. "You can't do this to us."

Sally's hands tugged at the hooded leader's shoulders. The latter snarled and pushed her away, the back of his hand striking her cheek and spilling her against the wall.

Rockett cursed and bolted toward the renegade. Another outlaw stepped in his path, gun leveled.

"Stay put, Rockett, or yuh'll get hurt!" said the outlaw.

The renegade leader said nothing, but his eyes gleamed maliciously at the girl. Sally recovered her balance and her fingers fled to her cheek, feeling the sting of the back-handed slap. There was a shocked disbelief in her face before it changed to anger and bitter scorn.

"It seems I made a mistake about you," she said quietly. Her shoulders were very straight, and she was more deeply hurt than she had ever been. "I should have let Kip Randall hang you."

The hooded renegade laughed, but the tall, broad-shouldered leader had nothing more to say. He gestured curtly to the man beside him. The latter nodded, and spoke to the glowering nesters.

"Outside, everybody! We aim to burn down this shack."

In the yard other voices could be heard, mingling with the slur of hoofs and the high-pitched squawking and fluttering of chickens. Guns were popping and coarse laughter drifted in out of the night.

Cursing and mumbling, Rockett led Sally out of the cabin. Mike Carew, Gordon and the others followed.

In the yard Sally halted and all around her the nesters growled in futile anger. Hooded outlaws were spurring their mounts back and forth through Rockett's truck garden patch, trampling the fresh vegetables. Two or three men had entered the chicken run and were amsuing themselves shooting at the chickens with their six-guns.

Near a stand of chaparral a mushroom of flame burst out of the small barn as the renegades set it ablaze. Ruby tongues of light weaved fantastic patterns through the gloom while the dry wood of the barn yielded to the fire's onslaught with a crackling roar.

"We'll leave yuh a wagon and a team of horses to get outa the country," said one of the outlaws, swinging to regard Rockett, whose face was chalkwhite and etched with deep lines of despair.

"Look like yuh've got me licked, Standish," whispered Rockett hoarsely. "But some day I'll come back to kill yuh."

One of the outlaws emerged from the cabin and called to the broad-shouldered leader.

"We've got the furniture in the middle of the room and everything's all set. Yuh really want to burn it?"

The broad-shouldered renegade started to speak, then stopped. Swiftly the man beside him spoke.

"There's a fire in the stove. All yuh have to do is up-end it."

Rockett cursed, his eyes dark with hatred.

"You afraid to talk? It's all right. Yore men gave yuh away, Standish. We know yuh, and even with yore voice muffled there's no mistakin' yore white stallion yonder."

Rockett pointed to a milk-white horse ground-tied some distance away at the edge of the brush.

Suddenly from a low ridge a quarter mile away a knot of riders stormed out of a thick stand of trees. They were lashing their horses into a full gallop down the slope, and a sheet of livid flame traveled before them as the rifles in their hands boomed thunderously.

Chapter Ten

Impelled by the tremendous weight of the flat boulder anchored to his right foot, Standish plummeted to the frigid depths of the brawling mountain stream. The shock of the icy water cleared his brain instantly, and he struggled against the downward pull of the rock which bore him deeper and deeper.

The blackness of the stream was a real thing—horrible and cloying—reaching frosty tentacles toward him. Pressure pumped at his ear drums, then he was jerked off his feet, rolling sideways along the rockstrewn bed of the branch.

The force of the plunge doubled his body in two so that his knees almost smashed his chin. His breath tore at his lungs, striving for release—a release that would bring water gushing into his system and ultimate oblivion for himself. He felt himself growing numb. The roaring in his ears became louder.

The agony of holding his breath threatened to tear his heart and lungs from his body. A vise had taken him in its grip, slowly choking him. It froze the blood in his veins, sent a surging sickness up from his stomach.

Then, with the water turning blacker and blacker about him, hope flared anew in his breast. There was a way—if he only had enough time!

Until this moment he had forgotten the knife concealed at the back of his right boot where the seam was doubled. But with his wrists lashed behind his back he might not be able to get at it. Standish's lips folded tightly and he doubled up his body. Desperately, his face turning bluer, his eyes bulging, ears ringing from the pressure of the water, he forced his lashed fingers into the top of his right boot.

He found the knife, gripped it awkwardly and dragged it clear. Sprawled in the icy depths of the creek, he hacked at the thongs that tied his ankle to the flat boulder.

His teeth clicked together when the keen blade cut his leg. Again he tried, desperation driving him on as the excruciating agony of failing breath bulged the walls of his lungs. Suddenly a slash of the blade cut through the rawhide. The weight dropped from his feet and like an arrow shot from a bow, Standish's body was catapulted to the surface of the stream, while the knife slipped from his cramped fingers.

Bouncing clear of the water, his mouth flipped open. The cool night air rushed into his lungs with soft, sweet pain. He bobbed about on the surface of the roaring creek and was shot downstream by the turgid torrent. Arms still lashed behind his back, he fought the branch, trying to stay afloat. A few yards away he saw Whitey struggling against the current.

The brawling creek carried horse and man around a bend, smashed Standish against a slimy rock where his fingers strove for a handhold, but lost it immediately. Whirling end over end, once under the water, then floating like a jigging cork on the surface, he was swept a half-mile down the rocky gorge.

Exhaustion was wearying his muscles. He kept twisting his broad wrists back and forth—pulling and tugging, feeling the rawhide give a trifle as the water got in its work.

The thongs were cutting into the flesh, turning it raw, but he gritted his teeth against the pain. At last, the rawhide gave enough for him to slide his wrists broadside. One hand hauled clear, then the other.

He swung around in midstream and cut toward the near shore. His hands cleaved the white-laced, foaming waves that flung themselves against him, inundating his face. Whitey had already gained the shallows and was stumbling up the bank.

A wave broke over Standish's tousled head. Another lifted him high. On its low crest, he lunged forward, hands and arms digging deep. He came against a bulging rock, clawed for it with splayed fingers. He swung himself into a little eddy, fell to his knees and plunged under again. Desperately he hurled his body forward again, propelling himself with powerful leg thrusts. He broke clear, slipped to his knees.

Although his heart was racing in a riotous tumult from the tremendous exertion that had drained the strength from his sinewy frame, he managed to claw at some brush along the bank. Somehow he hauled himself half out of the water, flung a leg upon the earthen shelf and dragged himself from the creek.

Then he fell flat on his face in the grass, and gave himself up fully to the complete exhaustion of the moment.

How long he lay there in a half stupor he did not know. For a time it seemed that he lapsed into a state of semi-consciousness. But at last he stirred, shook himself and rolled over on his back. With an effort he sat up, his mind beginning to function again.

Off to the east in the direction of his own ranch he could still detect a dwindling red glow in the sky which meant the fire there was dying out.

Whitey was grazing with dragging reins in the sparse grass lining the banks of the creek. Now Standish got dazedly to his feet and staggered to the stallion. For a moment he had to lean against the animal's withers before he could muster enough energy to climb aboard.

This was a return from the grave. He had never been closer to death, and the thought of those agonizing moments spent in the creek, battling for survival, turned his weary cheeks dark and unruly. But it was the memory of the hooded renegades who had thrown him into the creek that stirred his deep-seated passions.

They'd tried to kill him, tried to put him where no one would ever find his body again, but they hadn't succeeded. He wasn't a man who died easily. He was alive; he had his horse; and he had his gun. And more than that he had his iron will to carry him on against the renegades.

All the bars were down now. The outlaws had given no quarter and from this moment all mercy died in Lee Standish. It was war all the way.

He dreaded the thought of what he might find at the Falling S. That fire he had seen spelled complete ruin for him. But if any of his crew were left he'd gather them up to carry the fight to the renegades.

Swinging Whitey about, he headed him downstream along the brush-choked bank seeking a way out of the gorge. A half mile farther on a side canyon cut into the main creek gorge and Standish swung into this. He rode with a grim urgency now, anxious to return to the Falling S and learn the fate of the men he had left there.

A half mile farther on the canyon splayed out in a series of rolling foothills. Standish angled due east and kept on, the scarlet glow in the sky growing steadily brighter all the time.

Then as he raced past the last thickets of timber and came out into the open glade, an overwhelming numbness came into his muscles. He was looking upon a scene of desolation. Ahead of him were the charred, still feebly burning ruins of his ranch and outbuildings.

The barn and the bunkhouse were completely gone and only a few spars in addition to the stone chimney remained to show where the sprawling one-story ranch-house had been. Dark figures moved about in the yard, marching back and forth.

The sight turned Standish wary and alert. He was wondering if they were some more of the renegades when a rider plunged out of a stand of mesquite behind him.

"Lee! We thought yuh were done for. Where have yuh been?"

Relief flooded through Lee Standish when he recognized the redheaded Lynn Boyle. He remembered now that he had ordered Boyle to stay with the roundup camp in the North Hills. He should have been angry that his orders had been disobeyed, but he was not.

"Only luck kept me alive," grunted Standish. He looked out toward the ruins. "The blasted skunks made a thorough job of it."

Boyle nodded somberly and spurred his horse alongside Standish.

"Ben Fuller told me yuh ran into the polecats as they hightailed away from here. He told me about Dan Young gettin' his—"

Before Boyle could continue the two riders were in the midst of the Falling S crew racing back and forth across the yard. Standish's mouth settled in a thin, hard gash across his skin when he saw three prone bodies on the ground sprawled in the stiffened attitude of death.

Ben Fuller, a bandage about his head, and his shirt in shreds because a crude compress had been fashioned about his ribs where a bullet had torn into him, came forward. Beside him was Ed Gorevin.

"Lee, I'm glad to see yuh!" gasped Fuller weakly. "I saw yuh thrown off Whitey. I started to go back toward yuh when a slug creased my scalp and things went black."

There was a ruddy excitement in the old ranny's weather-seamed cheeks, and his eyes were full of concern for the Falling S owner.

"When I came out of it," he resumed, "the trail was deserted. All I could find was Dan Young's body. There was no one else, though I'm shore we drilled a couple."

"We did," agreed Standish tersely. "They must have taken the bodies away to prevent identification."

"But what happened to yuh? Yuh disappeared completely."

"They had me slated for a watery grave, but my number wasn't up."

In words that were bitter and vitriolic Standish gave an account of his plunge into Bald Eagle creek and his ultimate escape.

"The dirty skunks!" breathed Ed Gorevin, the Falling S ramrod. "Got any idea who those raiders are?"

There was a bright interest in Gorevin's face and his eyes bored into Standish's taut features.

"No," responded Standish, a dry irritation in his voice. "At first I thought it was Brad Buchan's bunch. Now I'm not so shore. I couldn't place the voice of the gent who was leadin' them, though it sounded a little familiar."

"It didn't sound like Chad Runyan?" demanded Fuller.

Lee Standish came out of his saddle with a leap that belied his weariness. He whirled on Fuller.

"Runyan? No. What makes yuh say that?"

"Well, it seems that when the skunks raided the place here our boys made it too hot for them and they didn't get a chance to carry two dead men back with them. Both of those men are Chad Runyan riders."

Wide jaws set like a steel trap, the young rancher moved to the dark mounds of two bodies. In the faint glow of moonlight he stooped down to examine the two men indicated by Ben Fuller. Black bandannas circled their throats, but their hoods had been removed. Standish had no trouble in verifying Fuller's statement that the raiders were Runyan men.

Slowly Lee Standish moved among the other bodies, recognizing the three punchers he had left in charge of the Falling S while the rest of the crew was busy with the roundup. They were all dead. Only Ed Gorevin had survived, and the latter had a bloody bandage on his left shoulder. Standish turned now to face Gorevin.

"How did it happen, Ed?" he demanded.

Gorevin cleared his throat uneasily, grimacing with pain as he moved his shoulder.

"I was just gettin' ready to ride back to the roundup camp when the buskies struck without warnin'," he growled. "Two of the boys were walking across the yard between the bunkhouse and the house and were cut down. They didn't die right away and they made it hot for the raiders with their guns before they cashed their chips."

Standish nodded stonily. He was looking at one of the waddies who was sprawled face down in the dirt, a round bullet hole in his back.

"Jenkins was shot in the back," he said, his face oddly intense.

"Yeah, I saw that," muttered Gorevin. "The buzzards rode a circle around the place. Reckon that's how he got it that way."

"Lucky yuh got away yoreself," observed Fuller.

Ed Gorevin bristled a bit at that. He glared at the old puncher, sensing in Fuller's remark a slight hint of suspicion.

"Watch how you talk, Ben," he said savagely. "I did what I could, but I figgered a live Falling S hand was better than a dead one. So I grabbed my horse and managed to ride clear into the brush. I saw them set fire to the place. Nothin' I could do to stop 'em."

Fuller started toward Gorevin but Standish stepped between them.

"If there's any fightin' to be done we'll do it against the right parties," he said grimly. To Boyle he added: "You should have stayed in the camp, Lynn."

"Yeah, but seein' that fire made me so blamed mad, I just had to take the boys over to see if we couldn't help. I left one man to guard the herd. But we got here too late."

"That man you left will be dead by now and I reckon the cattle are scattered in the hills." Boyle looked at him in haunted bewilderment. "Before they shoved me over the cliff," added Standish, "they told me their next move was to scatter that North Hills beef."

"That means yuh're smashed," said Ed Gorevin, his eyes dark and unreadable. "We'll never get another herd together in time."

"Of course we won't," said Lee Standish. There was a deadly timbre in his crisp voice that drew every Falling S puncher's gaze. "With no ranch and no cattle, we're free to roam the hills."

"What do yuh mean by that?" demanded Gorevin.

Standish's somber eyes glittered like gray stones in winter moonlight. There was a hint of desolation in his face, then it was lost in the turbulent sweep of headlong rage and resolve.

"Revenge!" he snapped. "That's what I'm after. We've got no ties. Those raiders have smashed us; they've threatened the nesters and they're ready to glut themselves on an unholy feast of this whole range.

"Every man here that's willin' to run the risk of winnin' a six-foot grave in boothill, but wants to throw in with me is welcome. I'm formin' the Legion of Vengeance. That's what we'll call ourselves from now on.

"I'm shore Buchan is behind those raiders and it looks like Runyan is, too. From now on we'll make this range tough for them to ride. They want trouble, so we'll carry it to them. We'll go to the roundup camp first, then send

Runyan's men back to his Double R. After that we'll see what we can do to raid Runyan's beef. We'll do the same to Buchan."

"It means the owlhoot," observed Fuller, rather dryly.

"Shore," agreed Standish thinly. "But those raiders have made the fastest gun the law here. Mebbe our Colts are a little faster. Let's ride. How many of yuh are with me?"

A low, grim cheer of universal assent greeted that question.

"I reckon if I had money now I wouldn't know what to do with it," grunted Ben Fuller. "So let's fight!"

"Ben," said Standish, "I'll need some fresh loads for my gun. My bullets got wet in the creek. Don't want to take a chance with 'em."

Fuller nodded and gave him a handful of bullets. Boyle and one or two others handed some of their surplus ammunition to Standish while he took the time to clean and dry his ivory-handled Colt.

Several horses had been salvaged from the fire and now the two dead renegades were loaded aboard horses and tied down. Then, the rest mounted and headed away from the still smouldering ruins. Lee Standish did not even turn to look back at this place which had been home. All his bridges had been burned and from now on he and his men would be on the dodge.

They were half an hour's ride away from the North Hills camp when the distant popping of six-guns was carried to their ears on the wings of a cool night wind.

"Those blasted outlaws again," growled Ben Fuller.

"Yuh may be right," said Lee Standish. "And that gunfire is comin' from the direction of the nester basin. Looks like the Legion of Vengeance has its first job all cut out for it. Come on!"

His voice lifting stridently through the night, Lee Standish kicked Whitey into a dead run. Behind him, riding silently but like grim harbingers of death, came the rest of the Falling S crew. Just ten men in all, daring hell and high water for a lost cause!

For six or seven minutes they stormed along the undulating twists of the trail while the shooting grew louder and more insistent. Charging to the crest of a low ridge they came out on a grim and lurid scene.

Down in the hollow of the basin's east end lay Jube Rockett's small homestead. And in the open ground below crimson flames were leaping skyward from a blazing barn.

Rifles popped into the hands of the Falling S punchers as they thundered down the slope. A wild yell burst from Ben Fuller's throat. His head throbbed from his recent creasing, but he was a tough old warhorse and gunsmoke was the elixir that kept him going.

Muzzle light lanced in bright red-yellow streamers from leveled Winchester barrels. In the basin the hooded raiders scattered toward cover and their own guns began to bark, but the range was short.

Halfway down the slope Standish spotted another white horse. He saw a hooded figure race across the glade and leap into the saddle, then yell something to his companions.

The night was torn apart by the booming, pulsating thunder of guns. The Legion of Vengeance struck the edge of the glade and now bullets whined closely about them. One of the men cried out in pain, but remained in the saddle. Rockett ducked inside the cabin and emerged with a rifle, then began pumping lead at the fleeing figures of the renegades.

"Close in on 'em!" roared Lee Standish.

Thrusting his smoking Winchester in the boot underneath the stirrup fender, he brought out his Colt and snapped two quick shots at a bolting renegade. He saw the man lift up his arms, start to reel out of the saddle.

But another renegade swooped in, lifted the fellow bodily out of the kak and thundered on toward the timber to join the rest of the band in flight.

The nester basin was full of sound. Bullets smashed into the log walls of the cabin, whined sibilantly through the air, slogged into the boles of trees. Standish saw the flash of a gun, laid his answering fire on that, then swung around toward Lynn Boyle.

"Lynn! Follow them. Get as many as yuh can!" he yelled. To Ben Fuller, he added: "Ben, stick with me!"

Then while Lynn Boyle was leading the other seven Falling S hands in a wild chase out of the basin, Standish returned to the cabin where Rockett, Carew and the others milled about in confusion.

"Standish! What kind of a trick are yuh tryin' to pull?" roared the grizzled old nester, swinging his rifle barrel around to cover the Falling S owner.

For a brief, shocked moment Standish read the naked hate in Rockett's eyes, saw the grim intent to kill in the whitening of the nester's fingers. Swiftly he fed steel to Whitey's flanks. The stallion lunged forward just as the rifle blasted. A hot blast of wind fanned past Standish's cheeks, then he sent the stallion plunging into the nester.

Whitey's powerful shoulders plowed into Rockett and knocked him to the ground, the rifle clattering from his hands. Nearby Fuller's gun bucked once and the gunman, Stone, dropped his forty-five.

"Hold it, all of yuh!" grated Standish harshly.

He stared down at Rockett who climbed to his feet, shaking his fist in the rancher's face. There was amazement and scorn in Standish's eyes, but anger was a stronger force, hardening his words.

"That's a fine way to show yore appreciation of our help," he told Rockett, his eyes bracketing the other with a cheerless intensity.

"I'd do it again," raged Rockett. "Yuh're foolin' no

one, Standish. It was yore men who trampled my garden patch, burned my barn. They even mentioned yore name, though you tried to shut 'em up!"

"How could I be in two places at once?" snapped Standish. "I saw that other white horse. I couldn't have been here, ridden off to the west as those renegades did, and at the same time come charging down yonder slope from the north to help you."

"Those jiggers are tryin' to frame yuh, Lee," said Ben Fuller. "And Rockett and the others here fell for it." Fuller regarded Rockett and Carew with ill-concealed contempt. "We should have left yuh be."

"I don't know why yuh didn't," growled Rockett intolerantly.

"Wait, Jube," said Mike Carew, his ruddy cheeks flushed. "Mebbe we did make a mistake. There were *two* white horses. I remember seein' one of those hooded jaspers run for the white in the basin while Standish was leadin' his own men on another white horse."

"We all saw that, father," burst out Sally fiercely. "You're being stubborn and unfair."

Now she ran to Whitey and looked up in Standish's face.

"Lee, I'm sorry," she said. "Like father and the others, I believed you were actually raiding us—until just now."

Breathlessly, she explained what had transpired in the cabin.

"Shore," interrupted Mike Carew. "I see it all now. That polecat called the leader 'Lee' purposely and the jigger pretended to get mad because his pard revealed the name."

"And that's why the leader kept his voice muffled and was afraid to talk," added Sally eagerly. "He knew that if he spoke too much we might realize it really wasn't Lee."

With Ben Fuller still covering the nesters with his guns,

Standish stepped out of the saddle. Immediately Sally came into his arms. An electric shock of excitement leaped vividly between them. It was something they couldn't control, didn't want to control.

Her body was warm and vibrant against his, and there was a sweet wild fire in her lips as they met his in a warm rush.

"Sally!" stormed Rockett. "I told yuh I don't want yuh to bother with Standish. Get inside."

Rockett's slender figure trembled with rage. Sally pushed slightly away from the Falling S owner, but she took his hand in hers and faced her father with a stubborn defiance.

"Father, it's time you came to your senses," she said quietly but sternly. "Lee has helped us tonight and he's tried to help us before. If it hadn't been for him our cabin would be in ashes. Before those masked raiders came you were saying you meant to fight them. Maybe with Lee's help you can fight with a chance to win."

"That's yore only hope, Rockett," said Standish, flashing the girl a grateful glance. "It's fight or die." His voice dropped, his face turning gray and morose with dismal memories. "Tonight another bunch of renegades burned down my ranch buildings and killed three men. By this time I reckon they've also scattered my beef herd in the North Hills after tryin' to anchor me to the bottom of Bald Eagle Creek."

"Lee! You don't mean that?" demanded Sally, a haunted look on her cheeks.

"It's true," murmured Ben Fuller. "They smashed us."

"But we're not licked," snapped Standish. His broad shoulders stirred in mounting fury and determination. "This attack on you is probably only the start of an all-out plan to drive you from the basin. Somebody is attempting to hog the whole range. We're not shore who it is, but the chase is narrowin' down. I figger it's Runyan or Buchan or both. Two of the skunks shot at my place were Runyan hands. They're the jiggers tied face-down on their saddles. I aim to send them back to Runyan for burial."

He broke off as Rockett and Carew, their faces stern and troubled, walked over to stare at the corpses on the two horses.

"I'm open to suggestions," Carew said tersely when he returned.

"Only one thing to do," murmured Standish. "Fight or run—and I'd rather fight any day." He stood there, a thoroughly dark and vital man, a prey to the rashness and the wildness that ruled his feelings. "With my men I've formed the Legion of Vengeance. Our purpose is to make the hills tough to ride for those masked raiders.

"Runyan seems to be in it, so we'll give him a taste of trouble first until we get to the bottom of this range deviltry. You gents are welcome to join us."

"Standish, I'm with yuh," declared Mike Carew.

"If we join yuh we'll be puttin' ourselves outside the law," grumbled mild Jim Holland.

"With Syl Manders gone, the only law is the law of the six-gun," intoned Standish. He paused, then added as if a sudden thought had come to his mind: "But there's one thing you nesters must do to protect yoreselves legally. You're all squattin' on government range. As squatters you technically have no rights unless yuh file homestead claims at New Benton. My advice is to take yore measurements of land area tomorrow, then ride to New Benton after dark and have them recorded."

"What good will that do?" Ace Gordon asked, his eyes blinking in unfriendly fashion at Lee Standish.

"I've already explained it'll legalize yore holdings. Even though the law doesn't amount to much here, havin' yore land claims on file will put the renegades that much more outside the law."

"That sounds like good advice," grunted Mike Carew. "I'll do as you suggest. When that's done I'm joinin' yore Legion of Vengeance."

"How about you, Rockett? And you, Gordon?" queried Standish.

A flicker of hope had lightened the gray-haired nester's features. Now as he glanced at Standish, his face grew stubborn again.

"I reckon I was wrong about this raid," he admitted gruffly. "I was so mad that I just couldn't see how things were. I realize now you couldn't have led those renegades."

He hesitated a moment and when he spoke again there was more intolerance in his tone.

"Yore advice about filin' a homestead claim is okay, but I'd rather not team up with yuh. I'm beholdin' to yuh already and I figger us nesters ought to handle this ourselves without gettin' help from cowmen. I aim to organize my neighbors to fight those raiders."

"Suit yoreself," said Standish, wheeling around at the sound of hoofbeats as Ed Gorevin and Lynn Boyle plunged out of the brush, leading the Falling S hands. He noted that they had no prisoners and that their horses moved with a labored tread.

"How did you make out?" he demanded.

"They got away," growled Gorevin with an angry grimace. "The jaspers had too much of a lead and their horses were fresher than ours."

"Too bad. I was hopin' yuh might have caught up with the skunk who was ridin' the white horse and posin' as me."

Repeating his warning to the sodbusters to file their homestead claims, Lee Standish led the Legion of Vengeance back toward the badlands.

At the North Hills camp they discovered that all the Falling S beef had been driven off. There was a welter of hoofprints from cattle and horses, showing that a large body of riders had raided the place.

Near a clump of chaparral sprawled the trampled, horribly mangled body of the puncher Lynn Boyle had left in charge of the gather.

"That's one more score against those blasted snakes," said Standish through lips that were a grim, relentless wedge against the growing wildness of his face.

Pausing only long enough to dig a grave for the dead waddy, the Legion of Vengeance moved on.

"I know a canyon hideout farther north where we can hole up," Standish informed the others. "Not much chance of it being found, and it's high enough to give us a view over the surrounding country. We'll go there as soon as we send these bodies to Chad Runyan."

When they reached a timbered ridge overlooking the Double R outfit, Standish signalled a halt. Taking out a stub of pencil from his pocket, he scrawled a message on a square of wrapping paper. Ben Fuller spurred to his side, his manner full of curiosity.

"Just a note to Runyan to let him know how things stand," the Falling S owner informed the oldster.

Fuller peered owlishly at the message and read it half-aloud:

Runyan:

A band of masked raiders burned my Falling S ranch last night, killed three punchers and drove off all my cattle in the North Hills. The two men accompanyin' this note were with the raiders and stopped too much lead.

The Double R can bury its own dead. Now that yuh're out in the open the Legion of Vengeance wants yuh to know that buryin' yore own men may get to be a habit.

Lee Standish

"That's tellin' them," breathed Fuller, his eyes glowing. "And that Legion of Vengeance will give 'em somethin' to think about."

Standish merely nodded and fastened the note to the saddle of one of the outlaws' horses. Then he slapped both animals on the rump and watched them clatter down the slope toward the dark bulk of ranch buildings.

Chapter Eleven

It was after midnight when the Legion of Vengeance arrived at the canyon hideout Standish had selected. Brush and rocks cleverly concealed the entrance. Towering gray walls lined either side of the gorge, and the far extremity terminated in a sheer, unscalable bluff.

Truly, it was an impregnable stronghold. A handful of men could defend it against an army. And the only access to it was by means of a narrow, boulder-lined trail that skirted a yawning abyss on one side and treacherous shaley slopes on the other.

Without bothering with the precaution of stationing guards on the high promontory that overlooked the hideout, the legion members rolled up in their blankets and fell into an exhausted sleep. But at dawn Lee Standish routed them out again.

Selecting two punchers from his small crew, he gave them what money he had in his pockets and instructed them to make the long ride into New Benton for some food supplies. He didn't wish to run the risk of sending them into Drayton.

The men left, taking along two extra horses as pack animals. The mounts were good riding stock, but for the time being they would have to be used to transport supplies. A buckboard would have been preferable but there was none available. And even if there had been, no flatbed wagon could have traversed this section of the badlands.

"Saddle up!" Standish directed the rest of the men. "We've got work to do today along the vengeance trail."

An eager murmur of approval rippled through the legionnaires as they threw their gigs on selected mounts and rode out of the concealment of the narrow defile.

A little more than an hour later they were on Double R range, keeping to the brush and timber as much as possible. They covered three miles of rolling hills before they came upon a large prime beef herd guarded by two Runyan punchers. Standish turned to Ben Fuller.

"Ben, take three men and circle that herd. No gunplay if it can be avoided, but I want you to capture that waddy on the south side. Lasso him, then slug him. Tie him to his saddle and send his horse off for home. We'll do the same with the jigger at this end."

Fuller nodded, his face rippling with pleasure.

"I'm gonna enjoy this job, Lee," he said and rode off with three men spurring in his wake.

Standish allowed a few minutes to elapse, then gestured to Gorevin, Boyle and the others to follow him through the brush. They crept up closer to the grazing herd which numbered several hundred head. The Double R puncher rode the edges of the herd unsuspectingly.

When the latter came within twenty yards of the stand of chaparral hiding the Falling S waddies, Standish sent Whitey plunging into the open, and bolted straight toward the Runyan man. The cattle spotted Standish at once and began to mill uncertainly. One of the animals let out a bawling protest, and the Runyan puncher hipped about in his kak, his hand dropping to a holstered six-gun.

That was as far as he got. Lee Standish's rope hissed through space and settled over the waddy's head and shoulders, pinning his arms to his side. Standish hauled in on the rope as Whitey stopped on a dime and braced his hoofs.

The Runyan man was dragged out of his saddle. He

fell in a heap on the ground. Standish dismounted swiftly and came up to his victim.

"Standish!" gasped the puncher, his breathing quick and shallow. "What are yuh tryin' to do?"

"I need yuh to carry a message to Runyan," Standish told him.

The puncher writhed on the ground and made another stab for his gun. Then it was that Standish stepped in and slugged him.

"Sorry, yuh forced me to do that," he murmured, though the puncher could not hear him. "All right, Lynn and Ed. Load him on his cayuse and tie him down so he can't get loose."

"What're yuh gonna do with him?" Gorevin wanted to know, a strange distaste showing in his eyes and in the curling line of his mouth.

A still savagery stirred Standish's craggy cheeks.

"Send him back to the Double R with my compliments," he intoned.

Once again Standish scrawled a message on a piece of paper and fastened the missive to the back of the puncher's shirt where it couldn't be missed. The note read:

Runyan:

You don't need these hombres to guard yore north herd 'cause we've scattered the beef in the badlands. This helps square accounts. More later.

The Legion of Vengeance.

Ben Fuller rode up, leading a horse on which the other Double R waddy had been thrown face down. Standish sent both animals clattering toward Chad Runyon's spread.

"Now we'll haze these critters into the badlands where it'll take weeks to round 'em up again," said Standish.

Swinging their rope ends, the Legion of Vengeance

moved in on the milling steers and started them moving toward the badlands.

It was hot, weary work, but by noontime the beef had been thoroughly scattered among a welter of tangled brakes and canyons. With that job accomplished, Standish ordered a short rest before moving down to Circle B range, where they surprised a larger bunch of Buchan riders. There was a little gunplay and one Circle B man had his gun shot out of his hand before the Falling S riders disarmed Buchan's crew.

Then, every man was loaded on his horse, securely tied to the saddle and sent back toward the home ranch. Afterward, the legion set to work with a methodical precision and scattered the Circle B beef. And, as in the case of Runyan, one of the punchers carried a note on his back containing the same veiled warning sent to Chad Runyan.

It was late afternoon before the Legion of Vengeance returned to the canyon hideout where the two men who had been dispatched to New Benton for supplies were waiting. Ben Fuller and Lynn Boyle immediately busied themselves preparing a hasty meal.

Refreshed by food and drink, the men lounged about until darkness placed its thick mantle over all the steep slopes and canyons. After a bright half-moon had climbed into the sky above banks of fleecy clouds, Lee Standish left the fire, moved to Whitey and saddled him.

"Where to now?" queried Ed Gorevin.

"I aim to take a ride down toward the New Benton trail and see if the nesters are really gonna try to file their homestead claims. Might be worth while to investigate on the off chance the raiders may have heard about their intentions and try to stop them."

Gorevin nodded, a tight smile wreathing his stern face. "Seems like a good idea. How about my ridin' on down toward the basin to keep my eye on things? With most of the menfolks ridin' off to New Benton, it might be a good chance for those raiders to burn out every sodbuster in the valley."

"Do that, Ed. Better take one or two of the boys with yuh."

Explaining to the others that he expected to return before midnight and warning them to stay in the hideout, Lee Standish rode off.

An hour later he gained a narrow, brush-choked bench that overlooked the main trail and got down from Whitey and prepared to wait.

Time dragged on with interminable slowness. He was about to give up the vigil, thinking that the nesters had for some reason decided against the move, when he was aroused by the distant beat of hoofs.

Looking off to the south he saw a small band of riders. Because of the distance he could not identify the horsemen, but he was almost positive they were the nesters. Then he saw something else that filled him with a vague sense of uneasiness.

The main road which consisted of a line of undulating hills and curves, at this point narrowed to traverse a mile-long gorge hemmed in by beetling rock walls. Standish was camped at the very beginning of the gorge on a rocky bench that formed part of the cliff-top. If he stayed where he was the nesters would pass seventy feet below him.

But now a mile away near the spot where the defile splayed out into rolling hills again, he saw another band of riders rushing silently out of the timber. They seemed to be heading directly for the cliff edge overlooking the road at its northern exit.

Something about those dark, speeding shapes told Standish they were the hooded renegades. If so, then Rockett and his neighbors were headed straight for a bullet ambush. Standish felt his throat go tight and dry at the thought. Then a slow surge of blood warmed his cheeks and recklessness stirred his headlong temper into violent action.

Watching keenly, he saw the second band of horsemen separate, half going to the far side of the gorge, evidently to hide among the boulders there, while the rest holed up on the same side as Standish.

Somehow he had to warn the nesters away from the almost certain doom that awaited them. Running to Whitey, he leaped aboard and galloped off along the bench in the direction of the outlaws.

When he saw the sodbusters entering the gorge behind him he flung himself down to the ground and quested among the rocks which lined the bench. A sudden desperate plan had entered his mind. It seemed the only way to save Rockett's men from destruction, even though he knew it would advertise his presence to the outlaws.

He came to a shoulder-high boulder perched precariously on the edge of the bench. Below it stretched yards of shaley slope ending in the narrow floor of the defile. Moving up to it, he thrust his weight against the huge slab, trying to shove it over the precipice.

Sweat studded his brow and all his muscles strained against his skin. The rock teetered forward under the impetus of his efforts, then swung back again.

Meanwhile the clatter of hoofs marking the approach of the nesters through the canyon increased to a growing clamor. Girding his strength for a final desperate attempt, Standish shoved with all the power in his shoulders and back. Again the boulder teetered precariously. But this time it went all the way over and careened down the slope.

Thunder boomed in the gorge as other rocks, loosed by the boulder, went cascading along in a monstrous landslide that filled the night with lashing beats of sound. Then Standish jerked out his six-gun and fired three times into the air.

Peering through the rising pall of dust, Standish leaned far over the parapet. He saw tons of rock jam into the defile, piling up a mountain of debris that would close the road for days. And just two hundred yards away the band of horsemen riding through the canyon, whirled their mounts in shocked astonishment, hesitated briefly, then raced at a dead run back the way they had come, sensing an ambush.

Abruptly Standish heard other horsemen pounding along the rock-studded mesa toward him. Then bullets began to drone through the air.

Jumping back from the edge of the precipice, Standish grabbed Whitey by the reins and dragged him behind the cover of a huge boulder. In almost the same motion he pulled the Winchester from the boot, thrust the butt into the curve of his shoulder and squeezed off a round of shots into the black knot of horsemen storming toward him.

The riders were approaching in a fan-shaped wedge with muzzle light winking redly from their fists. Most of their shots were going wild, ricocheting off the rocks, and Standish was having no better luck. But his deadly fusillade served to turn the renegades toward the timber to get out of range.

For a few moments both sides kept up a sporadic round of shooting. Then the outlaws made a charge across the open plateau that lay between the timber and the boulder field. Standish grimly stood his ground. Bouncing up to answer the volley of outlaw fire, he felt flying metal tug at his left cheek, heard the angry whine of other slugs buzzing through the air, overshooting their mark.

Then the Winchester in his hands throbbed and bellowed again. It was difficult shooting at those constantly moving targets, but with his last two shots he emptied two saddles. He distinctly saw two of the hooded raiders drop their guns and go tumbling into space from the saddles of their boogered mounts. Suddenly a strident voice boomed through the night.

"Ride, you fools! Let that jigger behind the rocks go! After those nesters and try to head them off."

Another volley of lead stormed through the rocks which sheltered Standish, before the outlaw crew whirled their mounts and swept off.

Chapter Twelve

Blood ran in a warm trickle along Standish's cheek, mixing with sweat and grime. At this moment he was thoroughly spent and weary, yet some dim reserve of energy kept him going. He was living on nerve—but it was an iron, unyielding nerve nurtured by deep-rooted hate and a terrible resolve that left him a man without any care for himself or the hard risks he ran.

Dust and gunsmoke mingled in a devil's fog across the land. Moving out from behind the protection of the boulders, he went at a lurching run across the mesa toward the two outlaws he had dropped with rifle slugs.

The first man he reached was dead from an ugly wound in the chest. Pulling off the dark hood, Standish looked at the hard, thin-lipped features without any recognition. The man quite obviously an imported gunslick.

Standish went on to the second outlaw, and jerked off the hood. Then a smothered exclamation burst from his lips.

"Ed Gorevin!"

Shock rolled through Lee Standish in a frigid, numbing tide. He gazed at the dark, taciturn features of his foreman, noting the faint lifting and falling of his chest that told him Gorevin was still alive.

The involuntary exclamation Standish uttered stirred Gorevin back to awareness and he opened his eyes. In the moonlight the ramrod saw Standish bending over him.

"Blast you, Lee," Gorevin gasped hoarsely, a bubble

of blood breaking on his lips. "Yuh're too lucky to be human. You—you should—be dead. We—tried to—smash yuh out—yuh're just too—"

"I never figgered yuh'd turn out to be a skunk," Standish said, an unholy rage pulling at his restraint. "They must have paid yuh well. Yuh've ridden with those raiders all the while?"

Gorevin coughed in agony and nodded.

"I reckon yuh're the jasper who was in the alley the night I brought Buchan and Randall to the Drayton jail," persisted Standish, forcing his mind into an ordered review of events. "You stole that poison and salt block, then got the raiders to rescue Buchan and Randall to break my case against them."

"Shore," whispered Gorevin, his voice coming fainter and with greater effort. "And yuh—never—guessed it!"

"That explains why yore horse was all sweated when I reached the North Hills camp," said Standish, his eyes boring into the other's face with a compelling force. "And I reckon that puncher who died with a hole in his back when those raiders burned down my ranch, got his from you."

Standish broke off and anger in him rose like a mighty lump of flame in his throat. He grabbed Gorevin, pressing his burning eyes close against the latter's face.

"Who's behind those raiders?" he demanded. "You must know."

Gorevin gasped, seeming to choke on his own blood.

"Go to blazes!" he whispered.

Standish swore savagely and started to shake the man. Then Gorevin's eyes closed. A horrible rattle sounded in his throat. His entire body was convulsed by a long shudder, then stiffened in death.

A forlorn sense of defeat assailed Standish. He had felt he was close to learning the identity of the man who was responsible for all the deviltry that threatened to consume the entire range, but to the last Gorevin had defied him.

Though the exchange of words between Standish and Gorevin had seemed to consume a lot of time, scarcely three minutes had elapsed since the outlaws had fled and Standish had come upon the ramrod's body. Now, as he hunkered there beside Gorevin, a desperate plan came to his mind and he grabbed the fold of dark cloth which had concealed Gorevin's features and slipped it over his own head.

The outlaws were abroad tonight and though they had been temporarily thwarted in their attempt to ambush the nesters, their pursuit of Rockett and his neighbors might well end in slaughter.

Therefore, Standish meant to do what he could to prevent that even though it meant playing a lone hand again. He cursed himself for not bringing his crew with him, but it was too late for regrets now. Besides, it occurred to him that by posing as one of the raiders, he might be able to learn the location of their hideout and who their leader was.

Nearby Gorevin's big black gelding was grazing with dragging reins. Standish climbed into the saddle though Whitey came trotting over to him, whinneying his protest. But, remembering that one of the outlaws had ridden a white horse, Standish realized he could not run the risk of riding Whitey now, for it would be a dead giveaway to his real identity.

Scarcely a mile ahead in the moonlight which bathed the mesa he could see the galloping shapes of the hooded raiders trying to close the gap between the nesters and themselves. Now Standish set the spurs to Gorevin's gelding and thundered off in their wake.

For fifteen minutes he rode at a breakneck pace, never letting the black beneath him slow up. He gained rapidly and as he swung around a bend he saw the raiders close in swiftly on three figures which seemed to have dropped behind from the main body of nesters. Guns boomed savagely and the flashes of those shots laid reddish pencils of light against the shadows. Then a voice that Standish instantly recognized cried out.

"Hold it! I'm not shootin' back. There's a girl here."

It was Jube Rockett! Standish felt his heart thump loudly beneath his ribs when he realized that for some unaccountable reason the nester had permitted Sally to accompany him on the journey to New Benton. Up ahead the shooting abruptly ceased while the hooded raiders closed in around the three figures.

Someone yelled a command and part of the outlaw band started away again to continue the pursuit of the rest of the nesters. Then those who remained behind whirled in their saddles, guns swinging around as Standish clattered up in a cloud of dust.

"Where did you come from?" demanded the nearest renegade.

"Put down yore gun," said Standish, keeping his voice hoarse and muffled. His insides were knotting and crawling with the expectation of being recognized, but he forced himself to go on. "That rifle shooter back in the brush winged me and got my horse. The jigger killed one of the bunch and I had the devil's own time catchin' up his horse."

Another rider pushed his mount close to Standish.

"I've got an idea that jasper back in the rocks was Lee Standish."

Surprise stabbed its hot glow through Standish's veins at the sound of that voice. He could have sworn it was the nester, Ace Gordon!

His eyes lifted to regard the renegade, and his pulse quickened when he detected the telltale blinking that always characterized Gordon's narrow-lidded eyes.

There'd been a traitor in the Falling S ranks and now here might be proof of treachery among the sodbusters.

Standish glanced at Mike Carew, Jube Rockett and Sally, wanting to throw himself at the outlaws who were shoving the nesters about roughly. It was a grim struggle, but he controlled his temper.

"Cut the palaver," said the tall rider in charge of the outlaws. "Let's get back to the hideout. I've an idea the boss will be glad to see these nesters."

Sally strained against the grips of two outlaws. Her face in the moonlight was white and tense.

Beside the girl Jube Rockett uttered a low exclamation of chagrin.

"I shouldn't have let yuh come along with us to New Benton, lass," he murmured dismally. "But I was afraid to leave you alone."

"It's not your fault, father," she cried. "If my cinch hadn't come loose we wouldn't have had to drop behind the others to tighten it."

The outlaw leader growled a gruff command to the crew and everyone moved to his horse and mounted. They proceeded at a rapid pace. There was no more talk and the outlaws seemed intent upon reaching their hideout without any further delay. They had covered about three miles when the band of raiders who had gone ahead to try to head off the nesters returned.

"The nesters outran us," informed one of the newcomers. "Once they entered Toro Canyon we quit the chase. In the dark they could hole up and pick us off one by one."

"The boss ain't gonna be glad to hear that," blurted the leader.

Twenty minutes of fast riding brought them to the outlaw hideout. Standish got down with the others in front of the lighted cabin, his glance flicking to the small barn some distance away. He began to think of Sheriff Syl

Manders, Slim Kawlor and Bob Reynolds and he wondered if by any chance they were being held prisoners in the barn or in this cabin.

Rockett and Sally were ushered inside and the rest of the crew trooped in after them. Standish blinked his eyes in the lamplight and found himself in a long room furnished with one or two crude chairs and a big table. At the table sat a bulky man and his eyes blazed with a tawny brilliance through the narrow slits of dark cloth hood.

Beside him stood Jess Hawley, the weather bureau man, completely unmasked. Seeing the man shocked Lee Standish to his vitals and started a bright flame burning in his eyes. The pattern of villainy was becoming deeper and more puzzling now that Hawley was inexplicably involved. What was Hawley's tie-up with the hooded raiders, and was he really a weather bureau official? Standish doubted that.

"We brought yuh three prisoners, boss," murmured the tall man who had led the raiders.

The dark hood of the man at the table lifted up and down and his right hand clenched in an odd gesture.

"What happened?" he asked quietly.

Despite the mildness of the tone there was a disturbing quality in the voice that got to the rest of the outlaws, turning them still and tense. Standish listened to the words and felt vibrations of anger rising through him. Here was the man who had consigned him to doom at the bottom of Bald Eagle Creek.

He remembered the spare, even voice with its haunting ring of familiarity. Desperately he strove to place it in his mind, but to no avail.

In his first encounter with this man he had come out second best even though he had escaped with his life. Perhaps this time the outcome might be different. Yet, looking at the group of men crowding the room he saw that the odds were practically insurmountable.

"They all got away except these three," said the outlaw in reply to the leader's blunt question. In halting phrases the man gave an account of the happenings above the gorge concluding with: "But the landslide worked in our favor, 'cause it forced those sodbusters to turn back."

"The point is they got away!" snapped the bulky man. For a brief moment his voice rose a notch, a feverish concentration entering it. "Did yuh get the man who shot at yuh on the mesa? It must have been Standish."

"No. He was cached behind boulders."

"Yuh're a pack of white-livered fools." Temper showed in the whitening of the chief's knuckles. "Standish must die. I'll give three hundred dollars to the man who delivers his dead body to me. With him dead that Legion of Vengeance he started will fold up. Tomorrow some of you will be assigned to scour the badlands for a sign of his hideout or any Falling S men. Others of you will watch the country near the New Benton road and see that none of the nesters try to reach the county seat."

Closely guarded by two outlaws, Jube Rockett strained forward.

"Who are yuh?" he demanded savagely. "Why don't yuh come out from behind that cloth hood instead of hidin' like a scared polecat?"

"Rockett," said the bulky man with no change in inflection, "I ought to kill you, but because of the girl I'll give you a chance to clear out for good—and I'll see you don't come back."

"Go to blazes!" fumed Rockett.

One of the renegades slugged the nester with his fist and the gray-haired man slumped against the wall. Sally uttered an outraged cry and started to move toward her father, but she was restrained.

For a moment a pregnant silence dropped upon the room. The only sound was the labored breathing of the gathered men. Then the bulky leader's head turned slightly and he addressed the outlaw who had directed the attempted bushwhacking upon the nesters.

"How many men did we lose?" he inquired.

"One man, according to one of the boys who got left behind for awhile when his horse was shot from under him," was the quick reply.

"That's all then."

"No, it's not all."

The speaker was the hooded outlaw whose voice so closely resembled that of Ace Gordon. Now the man swung about and strode toward Standish.

The blood in Standish's veins turned to liquid ice. The outlaw approaching him was looking at him with an odd intensity. Standish stood his ground, not a muscle quivering, though the sweat came out on his brow behind the hood that concealed his features.

Had his disguise been fathomed? Standish asked himself that grim question and could find no answer. He was aware now that the room had grown silent again. That stillness was a hideous thing, raking at the nerves of everyone in the room.

With an amazing swift motion the renegade's gun came out, jabbed into Standish's middle while his free hand lifted the hood from the young rancher's features.

"Lee Standish!" the man blared. "I thought so! Don't go for yore gun or yuh'll die."

Standish had made a frantic lunge for his holstered Colt, but he halted now as that round metal gun barrel prodded his belly.

"Take his cutter!" snapped the outlaw to a companion nearby, while a harsh murmur of astonishment slid about the room and the man at the table cursed softly in malicious triumph.

Standish felt his gun removed, and handed to the man who had unmasked him. The latter thrust the Colt in his belt.

"So you know me," murmured Standish, his face bleak and hard.

"Yeah," growled the outlaw. "The minute I spotted that yellow bandanna around yore neck I figgered yuh for an impostor. Mebbe yuh'll notice we all wear coal-black neckerchiefs."

"Nice goin', Gordon," said Standish with a sneer.

He saw a trace of dread enter those blinking eyes, then it was gone and Sally was turning her white, fear-wracked features toward him.

"Lee! Why did you take the chance?" she asked, her voice trembling on the thin edge of panic. "You were the man who fired those shots in the gorge and started that slide. And now—"

"And now I've bungled it," he finished dismally.

"Standish, this is really a pleasure," murmured the bulky man at the table. "You saved me trouble by coming here."

"Yeah," murmured Standish, his eyes bright and hard. "I aimed to find out where the gang's hideout was and who you are."

The renegade chieftain's voice droned on with a malignant, torturing softness.

"And all you've done is to reach the end of your string. The party is over and so is your luck."

He broke off and gestured to some of his hirelings.

"Four or five of you line up along yonder wall and draw yore Colts. Two more of you hold him by the arms. Hawley, you can clear out. I'll contact you later."

"You can't do that! It's—it's murder!" gasped the girl, as Hawley moved out of the cabin.

Sally tried to dart away from the outlaw holding her,

but he cracked her along the side of the face and she began to sob.

"You dirty dogs!" scowled Standish. "Leave Sally alone."

He, too, lunged forward but he was gripped firmly by two outlaws and shoved backward.

"All right, you men," resumed the renegade chieftain calmly as if there had been no interruption. "Take careful aim. Shoot when I give the signal."

Death was a cold and violent blast, buffeting against Standish. Once more he was thoroughly alone, for the gentle voice of the outlaw leader showed no quarter, and his gleaming eyes held no mercy. This was it, finally. Those six-guns would crash. Hot lead would tear into his body and that would be the end of everything.

His scalp began to crawl and his teeth went on edge. Yet, to all of these men Standish showed a gray-eyed indifference, a cold and withering contempt.

"Ready!" intoned the gentle, compelling outlaw voice.

"Yeah, we're ready to gun-shoot the first jasper that moves!" blared a harsh voice at one window.

"Drop yore hoglegs, you mangy sons!" snapped another command.

The bulky outlaw leader whirled at the table, his hand sneaking toward his holstered gun, then halting. The five raiders who were lined against the wall with leveled Colts seemed to have turned to stone.

"Ben! Lynn!" gasped Standish faintly.

As miraculous as it seemed, it was nevertheless true. Ben Fuller was at one window with two long-barreled six-guns menacing the room, his seamed face bleak and uncompromising. At the other window stood redheaded Lynn Boyle, likewise brandishing twin Colts.

"We've been watchin' the play, gents," said Fuller. "I'm all for salivatin' every skunk in this room just like you were figgerin' to kill Standish in cold blood. Drop them cutters!"

A second or two ticked by and the five executioners hesitated. Finally four of them let their guns clatter to the floor. Then, as other outlaws in the room moved restlessly, the fifth would-be executioner whirled and thumbed two quick shots at the hanging ceiling lamps. Darkness plunged down upon the cabin and bedlam broke loose.

"Sally!" roared Standish. "This way! Keep low!"

Even as he spoke guns began to boom, tracing reddish fiame patterns across the gloom. Lunging forward with a desperate surge of strength, he flung himself clear of the two renegades who had anchored his arms. His charge carried him into the outlaw he took to be Gordon.

Standish struck the man's chin with his head, distinctly heard his teeth snap together, then lost that sound in a rising clamor of guns.

The outlaw started to collapse, and Standish grabbed him about the waist, fumbling with awkward fingers at the man's gunbelt until he grasped his own Colt and dragged it clear.

Bullets sought him out, whispering past with a sibilant buzz. He stumbled against a diving body and swung his fist in a powerful arc, feeling his knuckles crack against flesh and bone. A man cursed and went down.

"Lee!" cried Sally, near at hand.

His hands fumbled through the darkness and he brushed the shoulder of her dress. Then he took her hand and whispered hoarsely.

"We'll make for the half-open door, but keep down."

"Hurry!" she urged. "Father's right behind us."

Men were yelling and cursing. Standish heard Rockett yelp in pain and knew the man had been hit.

At a spot near the door two guns were belching. Watching their flashes, Standish threw down on them. His weapon bucked and roared and immediately afterwards he heard high-pitched screams of agony, followed by the thump of falling bodies. Then he was slamming through the door and out into the yard with Sally racing after him.

They rushed into the shadows while Rockett and Carew followed. A dark shape charged away from the window. Standish's Colt swept up as Ben Fuller's voice lashed at him.

"This way, Lee! We've got horses and we've got Hawley!"

"Good! Don't let that weather expert escape!"

Just a moment they hesitated to fling a volley of shots at the front door, forcing the outlaws back. Then Lynn Boyle raced around from the other side of the shack. With him came three other figures.

"Who are they?" Standish demanded as they sped toward some ground-tied horses grazing under a stand of trees.

"It's Manders, Kawlor and Reynolds," yelled Fuller. "No time for talk now. We've got to ride. Here comes another bunch of outlaws."

From a cut in the hills to the south more riders were galloping. Now their guns began to flicker and Standish realized that any attempt to buck such overwhelming numbers would be plain suicide. As it was, they'd be lucky to escape without suffering casualties.

Under the trees Standish feverishly helped Sally into the saddle of a bay while he grabbed another animal. Ben Fuller assisted Rockett and Lynn Boyle lent a hand with the other three men, rescued from the hideout, whom Standish noted moved with an odd stiffness in their joints.

When they were all mounted they sent another fusillade at the outlaws in the cabin who were still lacing the brush with screaming lead. Then, reloading hastily, Standish, Fuller and Boyle turned their bucking weapons in the direction of that roaring knot of hosemen bolting toward them.

Standish saw those raiders start to swerve from the trail. Then Lynn Boyle spurred over to the bunch of saddled horses still remaining and cut their reins. With wild whoops and yells he cuffed them with his sombrero and sent them bucking and crashing toward the new renegade detachment roaring down the trail.

Riderless horses stormed into those mounted men and caused a milling tangle of bodies. Two outlaws were tossed out of their hulls. It was just the respite the Legion of Vengeance needed.

At a signal from Standish they all whirled their mounts and went pounding away from the hideout.

Outlaws began tumbling from the cabin. Six-guns boomed and angry pencils of flame followed Standish's crew until they were out of range and gigging recklessly across the rough terrain.

When twenty minutes had transpired and their horses were laboring, Standish called a halt to let the animals blow. He listened intently for sounds of pursuit, but heard nothing.

"That was close," he observed. "You gents came just in time. What brought you there?"

"Luck, I reckon," replied Fuller. "I was plumb worried about yore ridin' out alone again. Figgered you'd be headin' toward the New Benton trail to see that no bushwhack attempt was made against the nesters on their way to file homestead claims. Before we reached the trail we heard shootin'. By the time we got near enough we saw no sign of you, and the outlaws were pickin' up Carew, Rockett and Sally."

"There was no point in gettin' outselves killed buckin' the whole crew so we tagged along, never realizin' you were hidin' under one o' them hoods," added Lynn Boyle.

"I was a fool to play a lone hand," Standish grunted.

"If I'd taken all of yuh along we might have cleaned up that renegade bunch tonight. As it is, we had to beat it and it's a cinch they'll abandon that hideout now. They're still rakin' in the tricks."

"Not all of them," contradicted Fuller. "There's Jess Hawley. We cornered him as he was leavin' the shack. Mebbe he'll talk."

"I know nothing," blurted Hawley defiantly.

The weather bureau man had been guarded zealously during the headlong flight. Now his narrow, pale face was pinched with fear as Standish pushed his horse close.

"When I finish with yuh later you'll be glad to talk," Standish warned, his features gray and still. "You're comin' to camp with us." He halted, glanced at Sally. "In the meantime we've got to see you and yore Dad home safely, Sally."

"We'll be all right," said Rockett gruffly, but with a hint of reluctant admiration in his tone. "I reckon I owe yuh an apology for all the things I've said against yuh. What happened tonight definitely proves yuh're workin' to smash those blasted raiders. They've cleaned you out, yet yuh're fightin' to help the rest of us. From now on I'm with yuh just as soon as I can get the rest of the basin folks to file their homestead claims."

"Better leave that to me," cautioned Standish. "After tonight the raiders will probably be watchin' the woods trails to New Benton. I'll see yuh in the mornin'. Have all the data on area, location and landmarks for yoreself and all the rest ready for me and I'll take it to New Benton. One man will have more chance of gettin' through than an army."

"That's a good idea, Standish," said a new voice.

The Falling S rancher turned to regard the grizzled sheriff, who was flanked by the hay and feed man and the drugstore clerk.

"You still want to toss me in yore calaboose?" Standish queried.

Syl Manners smiled bleakly and shook his head.

"Not any more. Bein' locked up at that renegade hideout changed my outlook. That and the things I've managed to learn tonight. You were right when you said some jasper was tryin' to hog the range. My law don't count for a thing now. Things have gone too far. Right or wrong, I reckon I'm with yuh."

"That goes double for me and Reynolds," blurted Slim Kawlor.

"That's the spirit!" declared Lynn Boyle, grinning. "If yuh're wonderin' why Manders, Kawlor and Reynolds didn't join in the fight at the cabin, Lee, it's because their hands and feet were practically numb and useless from bein' trussed up so long.

"They had all to do to walk for awhile after we downed the two guards in the barn and released them. We'd have grabbed the guards' guns, but they dropped 'em in the hay and in the darkness we couldn't find 'em."

"Well," said Ben Fuller, "with Manders, Kawlor and Reynolds on our side it gives us three more gun-hands against those renegades. Ed Gorevin will be glad to hear about that."

Standish's cheeks darkened in a black tide of memory.

"Gorevin's dead," he told them. "He was one of the outlaws. I killed him tonight above the New Benton trail."

"Holy cow!" gasped Boyle. "I can't believe it."

"He admitted it before he cashed," said Standish. "He was the jasper who stole that evidence I had against Buchan and Randall. And either he or Ace Gordon tipped off the raiders that the nesters would be takin' the trail to New Benton tonight."

"What do you mean, Lee," asked Sally suddenly, her face puzzled. "That's the second time you mentioned

Gordon. I remember your calling that outlaw who unmasked you by the name of Gordon."

"I figger he's doublecrossin' the nesters," said Standish. "His voice sounded just like Gordon's and he had the same blinking eyes. Rockett, was he ridin' with you fellows tonight?"

A grave taciturnity filled Jube Rockett's cheeks.

"No. Gordon said he was goin' to wait before filin' a claim. It could have been him." Rockett paused a moment, his eyes swiveling from one to the other as if he were debating some decision, then resumed.

"Standish, you're the only one who knows about the gold I've been pannin' along the creek near my place, but we're all in this together and I might as well talk. The raiders have busted yuh and if this fight goes on we're goin' to need grub and money. I'm offerin' what gold I've got cached to you now. It don't amount to much, but mebbe you can use it to hire some gun-hands."

Lee Standish shook his head.

"Thanks, but I'd rather fight those huskies with the men we have. If I were you, I wouldn't tell anyone else about that gold. Men will do a lot of things for gold—even yore best friends—so be careful."

Standish paused and let his glance slide grimly around the group.

"Lynn," he said tersely, "take the boys back to camp and watch Hawley closely. Me and Ben here will see the Rocketts back to the basin."

Jube Rockett started to protest, but the nester saw that the Falling S owner would not be denied. Accordingly, they split up, one party heading north for the badlands; the other going south toward the basin. They had been riding about fifteen minutes through the darkness when Standish twisted in his saddle to address the nester.

"Rockett, I've been thinkin' that after what happened tonight the showdown will come soon—probably tomorrow night. Those renegades want the whole range—to build a cattle empire or for some other purpose. So far they've been balked. My bet is that they'll wait till late tonorrow night and attack you fellows and try to drive you out."

"What will we do?" put in Sally tremulously.

"Just this," said Standish, but directing his attention to the girl's father. "When you make yore rounds to get that land data from yore neighbors, tell them to pack up their belongings and move to yore place."

"But what for?" demanded Rockett.

"Join yore forces for protection. Separated as you fellers are, the outlaws could raid you one by one and destroy the basin. But if you all take refuge in one spot you can band together enough men to give 'em trouble. Keep the women and children inside the cabin. I'll arrange to have my crew hidden in the brush above the basin. If the raiders strike we can trap them between two fires.

"Instead of scourin' the hills huntin' the skunks, tryin' to raid the Circle B or the Double R, we'll let them come to us. They'll come—I'm shore of it—only we'll be prepared. Get every nester you can, but warn them to ride to yore place after dark so there's less chance of them bein' spotted."

"Sounds like a good idea, Standish," agreed Rockett gruffly. "I'll do what I can—and I hope yore plan works."

Nothing more was said for a while. Gradually Standish and Sally drifted ahead of the others, drawn together by an invisible magnetic attraction for each other.

"Lee," Sally whispered, her face white and strained in the darkness that cloaked the trail, "what's going to happen to all of us?"

"Yore guess is as good as mine," he answered gently. "But this I know—we're in for a fight. And whether we want to fight or not, there's certain to be trouble. I figger it's better to fight it."

He said it simply and without affectation. Some iron quality in him, the hint of rigid determination in his tone, pulled her glance to his face. It was a cleanly chiseled face, bronzed and rugged, but gaunted now by strain and weariness.

Sally's heart went out to this man who was so big, so self-sufficient, so hard and resolute—yet lonely in his stolid defiance of a range that was pitted against him.

"I hate to think of the hours ahead of us—and of the bloodshed that's sure to come. If there were only some way—" She broke off, at once aware of the hopeless trend of her own musings. Then her slender hand reached out to cover his while their horses drifted closer. "Lee, I wish you wouldn't go alone to New Benton. Something may happen—"

"It's the chance I have to take," he told her. "Besides, one man would attract less attention than a big group. Does it mean so much?"

He had his answer in the quick, courageous lift of her chin, the warm and ready smile on her lips, and in the increased tempo of her breathing. Her nearness, her shining loveliness, made his heart beat stingingly. He wanted to take her in his arms, and his hunger and his need of her was thoroughly clear to her in his eyes.

There was something about this girl that filled him with a sense of completeness. He found a strength in her, a heady power that was as strong and potent as wine. Although one corner of his mind was considering the dark and uncertain hours that lay ahead, he could push those thoughts from him now, and for this brief interval he was content with her presence warming him as nothing else could have done. For this brief interval he was at peace.

"Be careful for my sake, Lee—and—come back to me," she pleaded softly, her lips almost against his cheek.

"I'll be back, Sally." There was a strange dryness in his throat and speaking was suddenly difficult. "Nothin' will stop me."

Standish was reluctant to have the ride come to an end. But at last, they reached the basin and Standish gave Sally directions for reaching the hideout in the event of some unforeseen emergency. Impulsively, then, the girl spurred her horse close to Standish and put her arms around his neck and kissed him with a fervor and passion that matched his own. Then she whirled her horse and cantered around the cabin and was gone.

The ride back to the hideout seemed endless to Standish and Fuller. Both had been silent and morose, occupied with somber thoughts. But at last they rode into camp and found the entire crew out of their blankets awaiting their return. Boyle had told the men what had occurred at the outlaw camp and now they watched Standish unsaddle Whitey, turn him out to graze, then come back to face the cringing weather bureau expert who was being closely guarded.

"Have you made up yore mind about talkin' yet?" he demanded.

The weather bureau man stubbornly shook his head. Standish's mouth set grimly and he unbuckled his gunbelt. He took three strides and hit Hawley flush on the jaw with a looping left. Hawley staggered backwards, lost his balance and toppled to the floor of the gorge.

"Get up!" ground out Standish, his big, broad-shouldered frame appearing to take on weight. "Tonight, I'm findin' out what's back of those raids and who the man is that's directin' 'em."

Stooping down, he jerked the weather man to his feet and struck him solidly again, knocking him against the canyon wall. Anger rushed up out of Hawley, then, and he began to fight with a feverish desperation.

He lunged away from the wall, drove his knee into the

pit of Standish's belly. Standish gasped and started to double over. Hawley hit him behind the neck with a rabbit punch that dulled his brain and left him reeling. Hawley waded in, crowding the Falling S rancher across the shalely ground, butting and kicking.

Now all the accumulated bitterness that had gathered within Standish turned him wild and berserk, made him forget his pain.

Hawley tried to knee him again, but Standish leaped aside, then plunged in close, ripping the other with a hard left and right under the heart. Hawley gasped. He dropped his guard. Standish, waiting for just such an opportunity, pounced upon him and shot home a right to the jaw.

The minutes that followed were not pleasant to watch. Standish fought with the cruel and relentless precision of a machine. Three times Hawley went down under his powerful triphammer blows. At last, his face cut and bleeding, and reeling dizzily from punishment, Hawley lifted his hands in token of surrender.

"I'll—I'll talk," he gasped. "I've had—enough."

"All right," snapped Standish, breathing heavily, his fists still knotted. "What's behind those raids and what's yore game here?"

Through puffed, swollen lips Hawley mumbled his answer.

"I'm an advance agent for the railroad at New Benton," he said. "We've been keepin' it quiet, but the road is plannin' to build a spur to Drayton. I was sent ahead to buy up land as cheaply as possible. The right of way will go through the Falling S, the Circle B, the nester basin and other outfits, I expect."

Shock and understanding flowed through Standish's veins. The stake here was much larger than he had suspected. One man knowing about that railroad spur and securing all the land by force or guile, could sell the right of way at a huge profit.

"I see it now," murmured Standish tersely. "The jasper behind those hooded raiders found out about that spur—which is the reason for all the hellin'. I reckon you made some inquiries, figgerin' on contactin' the right man and gettin' a cut on the profits. Who is the leader of the outlaws? Adam Brill?"

Hawley gave a surprised start. But to Standish who was watching intently, he could not discern whether the railroad man's features showed a glint of guilt or not.

"Brill?" Hawley repeated, his teeth biting into his lower lip. "No—it couldn't be."

"What do you mean—it couldn't be?" snapped Standish. "I recall that Brill was the one who introduced yuh around the range. You're supposed to be his friend. With him ownin' the bank and mortgages on some of the spreads he'd be in a key position to profit by knowin' ahead of time about that railroad spur which will triple the value of the land."

"You're right about the railroad raisin' the value of land here, but Brill is not yore man," insisted Hawley with a strange note of conviction in his voice. "Even Brill thinks I work for the weather bureau. When I go out to meet the gang he thinks I'm ridin' to gather weather data."

"Yeah?" Standish was skeptical and angry. "How did yuh get in with those owlhooters, then?"

"Before I came to Drayton I received an unsigned letter statin' that the party knew all about the proposed spur and askin' me to meet him at the outskirts of Drayton a certain night at midnight if I wanted to make myself a nice wad of money."

"You're tryin' to make me believe, then, that through a leak in the railroad organization someone learned about the spur and lined you up in the deal?" snapped Standish. "Where's that letter?"

Standish never expected Hawley to produce the missive. But to his astonishment the railroad man reached into a pocket of his shirt and brought forth a much-creased and folded envelope from which he removed a yellowed sheet of paper. Standish read it and found the contents to be just as Hawley had stated. There was no signature and the handwriting, which was obviously disguised, was unfamiliar to him.

"How much are yuh gettin' outa this?" Standish inquired.

"Twenty thousand dollars—after the gang has all the land."

"And the first time you contacted this man he was wearing a black hood?"

"Yeah. I've never seen any of the men unmasked."

Standish scowled and gestured to Fuller.

"Ben, take Hawley away and see that he's guarded. It's time we grabbed some shuteye."

Although he was weary and needed sleep, the turbulent nature of Standish's thoughts kept him awake long after the others had dozed off. He kept considering Hawley's revelations and somehow he could not rid himself of the belief that Adam Brill was tied in with the outlaws.

Of all the men on the range the banker was in the best position to profit by taking over the land, since he held mortgages on most of the spreads. Yet, Standish could not deny that Hawley had seemed sincere when he stated that Brill was unaware of his, Hawley's, double life.

But if Brill was not the leader of the raiders, then who was the man? That question was one Standish could not answer, and he began to regret more and more that it had been impossible to force a showdown at the outlaw hideout.

Chapter Thirteen

Early the next morning Lee Standish stopped off at Rockett's place and learned that the nester had gotten the necessary data from most of his neighbors which Standish needed for filing homestead claims. He was surprised to learn, however, that a few of the sodbusters still distrusted him and had decided to make the journey to New Benton themselves later in the day despite Rockett's warning that they might encounter trouble in the wastelands.

Reaching the spot where the New Benton trail entered the mile-long gorge which had been the scene of the attempted ambush, Standish found Whitey grazing in the brush. He switched horses at once, then spotted two riders patrolling the higher hills.

Deciding that they were members of the outlaw gang stationed at strategic points to prevent any Legion men or nesters from reaching the county seat, he took a side trail through a dense stand of mesquite and manzanita. Bushes tore at his face and arms and lashed Whitey's sleek flanks.

The brush soon was replaced by trees which marched in a close and orderly line toward a high ridge above Standish. Deep in the corridors of the pines, he moved through shadowy darkness, punctuated now and then by patches of glaring brightness as the sun pierced the overhanging green canopy.

Pine needles muffled the sound of the stallion's progress as Standish climbed along the right flank of those two patrolling horsemen.

Reaching the crest of the ridge, Standish halted a moment to let Whitey blow. He twisted around in the kak to glance back through the trees. The woods were empty and the only sound was the whirling flight of a cowbird in the trees off to the north.

When he proceeded along the ridge to a line of boulders that reared their rugged shapes like motionless sentinels along several barren stretches, he saw the outlaws a considerable distance below him and looking in the other direction.

Reasonably certain, then, that the way ahead of him would be clear, Standish swung Whitey back to the narrow trail, angling directly toward New Benton.

After another four miles the timber thinned out and he found himself traversing rolling rangeland again, dotted with gentle hills lushly covered with grass and occasional brush patches.

The brassy ball of the sun climbed high in the sky, bathing the land in its searing heat. Waves of that heat danced in front of Standish. He was weary and his mood was grim and determined. Then heat and the glare of the sun had narrowed his eyes, shutting out a portion of his saturnine humor. But nothing could hide the bright gleam of impatience and the thrust of his stubborn will which remained in the somber depths of those eyes.

He had a job to do—in New Benton and back on the Drayton range. And until that job was completed—until the Legion of Vengeance had carried out its set purpose of smashing the organized lawlessness that threatened ruin to ranchers and nesters alike—he would know no peace.

It was past noon when Whitey carried his silent, taciturn rider into the north end of New Benton. To the casual glance it was like any other sleepy cowtown except that it boasted the added prosperity of a railroad and a long line of cattle shipping pens which dotted the siding beside the weatherbeaten depot.

Several men lounging about on the station platform gave Standish a cursory glance, then went back to their early afternoon dozing. Past the depot the main street with the dust hock-deep between the rickety board walks began to take shape.

False-fronted stores and shacks, their frame sides ravaged by wind and rain and sun, thrust their ugly shapes toward the brassy glint of the sunlight. Very few people were abroad in the town, yet every man watched Standish with a half-speculative attention.

He rode past the Mercantile, a barber shop, several feed barns and a blacksmith shop. Several horses stood hip-shot at a saloon hitch rack. As Standish drew abreast of the barroom the batwings flew open and a broad shouldered man stepped out on the narrow porch. For a moment his heavy-browed eyes lingered upon Standish with a hard and searching intensity.

Standish met the man's glance levelly, his attention registering certain significant details of the man's appearance. He had a harsh, bony face with a stubble of black beard covering his gaunt cheeks and narrow chin. He was tall and stood in a half-crouch, elbows hooked, hands like claws above the holstered guns which were snugged against his thighs.

He was a rough, untamed man and there was the look of a paid gunslick about him. Something about the ominous look of those guns, the calculating shrewdness of the tawny eyes and the studied casualness of the man's action in moving down to the walk sent a faint premonition of peril slicing through Lee Standish.

A queer, straining intensity flowed into his muscles and his left hand tightened imperceptibly on Whitey's reins. He had his quick and searching look up and down the street, then. Several men lounged on tilted-back chairs on the high veranda of the New Benton Hotel. But their interest in him appeared to be purely casual.

It was the gun-hung man who had stalked out of the saloon, and the black-garbed idler leaning against the wall of the livery barn diagonally across the street who occupied Standish's attention.

For a moment both men seemed to gaze past him, their eyes meeting in some silent exchange of impressions. Then the man by the livery tossed a cigarette butt into the dust and crossed the street behind Standish. His eyes were bright and greedy as they slid from the young rancher to the white stallion.

Twisting about in the saddle, Standish saw the second gunman pass within a few feet of the first man, then halt to thrust a shoulder against a porch post of the saloon. Standish imagined he saw their lips move though they were not looking at each other. But he was too far away to be certain of that.

Yet, the seed of doubt and apprehension had been sown within him, and he had his taut moment in which to wonder if these two men were also members of the renegade group which had been terrorizing the range. If they were, had they been planted in New Benton to take care of him in the event he got through the patrolling riders? And would they make an attempt to stop him from registering the nesters' homestead claims?

These were questions Lee Standish couldn't answer. But they placed a narrowing suspicion into his bleak, taciturn eyes. He put a hand down to his holstered gun to free it from saddle crimp. The threat of trouble was a growing torment in his mind, and the silence in this town was like a chill wind blowing up and down his spine.

Once again he was impressed by a feeling of utter loneliness. He was one man in this town—a town that was not friendly to him, yet not definitely hostile. He had braced himself solidly against the onslaught of the hooded raiders, and now was he riding into a trap of his own making?

There were men who knew him in New Benton—Judge Hawley and Clyde Zane of the Mercantile and Jim Heggel, the hotel owner. Yet, instinct told him he could expect no help from them if trouble broke.

Standish jogged past several more saloons until he spotted the one-story office of the town clerk which was separated by a narrow alley from the two-story courthouse and jail.

There was no hitch-rack in front of the clerk's office so Standish looped Whitey's reins about the rail in front of the courthouse and strode along the walk to the frame shack.

A slender, furtive-eyed man looked up from the long counter taking up half of the rear wall, at Standish's entrance.

"My name is Standish and I want to file some homestead claims," said the Falling S owner without preamble.

"For yourself?" the clerk inquired.

"No. For some nester friends of mine over in Drayton."

The town clerk stiffened as if he'd been slapped with an open palm. His eyes turned dark and brilliant, and he rubbed his hands together nervously, while he stared beyond Standish out toward the street.

Standish turned slowly and casually to follow the man's gaze, but the street was empty.

"Well?" he demanded harshly.

"I'm sorry," said the clerk quickly. "But you can't file for anyone else. Yore friends will have to appear at this office themselves."

Standish leaned forward. He placed his palms on the counter and when he spoke again he let his words fall slowly and deliberately, and no one could have mistaken the iron purpose in them.

"Friend, who are you tryin' to bluff? There's no such rule. Get out yore record books. I ain't got all day to waste here. I've got the necessary information about section measurements and their location with me. Yore job is to record them."

Grayness crept up into the clerk's narrow cheeks. He licked his lips nervously and could not meet Standish's burning stare.

"Yeah, shore!" mumbled the clerk. "I'll do that." He started to back away toward the corridor which led to a smaller rear room. "But you'll have to wait a minute until I run over to the courthouse to get my record book. I left it in Judge Hawley's office."

Suspicion flared up within Standish. But before he could lunge forward to restrain the clerk, the latter had darted out from behind the counter and had rushed through the rear room. Cursing under his breath, Standish heard the slam of the outer door, then silence flowed in, ominous and strained.

He did not trust the clerk. His manner had been too furtive, his shock at the revelation of Standish's mission too great to be casual. As the seconds dragged by with an interminable slowness, he began to regret letting the clerk out of the office. In fact, he wondered at the wisdom of making this hazardous trip alone.

Finally the rear door slammed again. Boots moved hurriedly along the puncheons, then the clerk appeared again with a thick ledge book under his arm.

"Sorry to keep yuh waitin'," he grunted.

The fear had left him now and Standish thought he detected a scheming speculation, a faint note of ill-concealed anticipation in the clerk's manner.

"I want to file homesteads for these men. Here are

their names and the location and areas of their holdings," Standish told him with a rising impatience over which he had no control.

He threw down several sheets of paper. The clerk took his time making the notations on a fresh page of the record book, at the same time marking off and tabulating the areas on a large map.

Each passing minute in the small office built up the pressure riding along Standish's nerves. At last, the clerk finished and closed the record book.

"I'll take receipts for those claims," Standish said tersely.

The clerk looked up, his eyes furtive again and sliding past Standish's shoulder, then coming back to the rancher's features.

"I can't do that," the clerk told him. "It's the policy to send out a representative to examine the area and verify the quarters filed upon. That'll be done next week."

A disgruntled frown ridged Standish's brow and he was about to voice a protest when he heard the scuff of boots behind him. He turned swiftly, arms lifting, his manner altogether alert.

The tall gun-hung man who had watched his progress from the saloon entered and sauntered over to the counter, thumbs hooked in his crisscrossed cartridge belts.

"I'll be with you in a moment," the clerk told the newcomer as he fumbled with the map on the counter.

"Take yore time," came the drawled answer.

There was a hint of sardonic amusement in the hard-faced man's eyes as he turned to regard Standish. He made no hostile gesture, yet the smell of evil was a sudden, disturbing presence in the office. It blew solidly against Standish. But he braced himself and strode to the door. He took one step outside, his keen glance sliding to the hitchrack in front of the courthouse, then he halted. Whitey was gone!

He had left the stallion tethered to the twisted locust pole, but now the animal had vanished. Standish's muscles turned rigid while hot blood began pumping in his head.

Chapter Fourteen

This was it! The trouble he'd been expecting was about to break. That knowledge was a sure, hard thing. He didn't need a diagram to realize that Whitey hadn't walked off by himself. Someone had led the animal away —to leave him afoot and helpless in this town!

Escape was cut off now and this was a trap. Underneath the quiet and serenity of New Benton sinister, unseen forces were gathering in an ugly manner to overwhelm him.

Standish's lips flattened in a thin wedge against his teeth while he stood immobile with a dark track of uncertainty clouding his vision. Then he whirled back toward the office and his bleak, sun-bronzed features mirrored the headlong surge of wildness that had its way with his feelings.

He came back with long strides into the room and halted three steps from the counter.

"Friend, I'll trouble you for my horse," he snapped.

His voice was even and controlled, but all the more dangerous because of it. His eyes were like chips of ice when they settled on the gunman.

"Yore horse?" the latter queried gently. "Don't reckon I understand, stranger."

The anger within Lee Standish grew to a steady, mounting vibration. It crowded all softness out of his speech. He swung around so that he faced the gunman and the clerk, yet at the same time had a side view of the street.

"I left my horse in front of the courthouse," murmured Standish through his teeth. "He ain't there now and I know he didn't walk away by himself. There's something wrong here and—"

"You've got things tabbed plumb correct, Standish," said a harsh voice behind him.

Standish spun towards the back room, his right hand sliding to his holster, then halting as his palm hit the smooth ivory stock.

"Keep yore hands at yore side and don't move!" came the swift warning.

Standish's cheeks darkened, and he looked with rigid concentration at the man who stood in the doorway, a six-gun lined on his chest. The newcomer was the man Standish had seen in front of the livery and who had crossed the street in back of him. It was obvious that, while the first man had occupied his attention and while he, Standish, had been discovering the disappearance of Whitey, this second gunman had circled the office to sneak in through the rear entrance.

"Since you know me, I reckon you gunsels are workin' with those hooded renegades," said Standish, bitterness and scorn edging his voice.

The man with the gun grinned. It was as wicked and brutal a gesture as Standish had ever seen.

"Yore guess is as good as mine," he drawled.

Knots of muscles stood out along Standish's jaw and the points of his shoulders were pressing against the taut stricture of his shirt. He glared at the first gunman who was rocking back on his heels, his thumbs still hooked in his cartridge belts. And the county clerk stood with his hands resting on the counter, a smiling uneasiness showing in his gaunt face.

"I reckon I was a fool for lettin' you outa this office," Standish said to the clerk. "You probably had that record book right in the back. When you pretended to go to the courthouse, you went to notify these jaspers that I was here. Who's yore boss, Buchan or Randall?"

The clerk started nervously and his eyes dilated, but he made no reply.

"For a gent that hasn't got long to live you're certainly plumb curious," murmured the man with the gun.

He spoke casually as if he were commenting on the weather or the current price of cattle on the Eastern markets. But Standish did not miss the significance of his words. He was at the end of his rope and he was meant to understand that.

"Me and my pard are new in these parts," said the man with the gun. His dark eyes glowed feverishly and his thin lips were drawn down at the corners. "When we saw yore white horse we figgered you were Standish, but we weren't sure, so we waited for the tip-off from the clerk here."

"You made a mistake comin' here to New Benton," said the first gunman. "Mebbe you didn't realize yuh're buckin' somethin' that's a lot bigger'n you are."

"I know this," snapped Standish, fury making his voice sound like the crackle of a whip. "You're two low-down skunks. I don't know who's ramroddin' yore mangy outfit, but yuh can tell him that he'll never gain control of the range until he wipes out my Legion of Vengeance. We aim to make the hills tough to ride for you buscaderos."

The first gunman laughed in derision and it was an evil sound to hear. Out of the corner of his eye Standish saw two townsmen saunter past the clerk's office, but they merely looked in and did not stop. The gunman had his Colt close against his hip, his own body concealing the weapon from anyone who might look in.

"Understand, there's nothin' personal in this," the first gunman resumed. "It's just that you stand in the way of the gent that gives us our orders. He's got big plans for the Drayton range and you made the mistake of buckin' them."

He wiggled his gun slightly and came forward between Standish and the other hardcase. Now he brought the Colt up in front of him.

"The three of us will be takin' a little pasear on horseback," he said. "In the badlands you'll have an accident. That's all. We'd do it here to save time, but it might cause too much commotion." He paused and spoke over his shoulder to his companion. "Jack, you take his Colt."

An icy wave of futility swept over Lee Standish. The serene, and casual brutality of these gunmen amazed him. They were cold and hard and utterly without sentiment. Their attitude had the county clerk wide-eyed and staring.

But if they expected Standish to exhibit fear they were disappointed. Desperation thinned his lips and narrowed his eyes, but his features remained taciturn and unmoved. And now because he was never a man to back down, because it had always been his policy not to walk around trouble when he could meet it head-on, he made his break for life and freedom.

Even as the first gunman started to walk away from the counter to remove his gun, Standish flailed his arms backward, the palms slapping the wall. Simultaneously he braced himself there and his right foot arced upward in a blur of speed. The outlaw close to him tried to step clear, but Standish's boot smashed against his wrist, knocking his Colt out of his hand.

Then Standish drove forward, slugged the renegade on the point of the chin with a looping right. There was the crack of bone meeting bone. The outlaw toppled backward and crashed into his companion. Their bodies tangled and both fell to the floor.

The second man landed on his shoulders and rolled over, his right-hand gun streaking into his fist. Muzzle light bloomed from the round, dark bore of the weapon, and a bullet smashed into the wall behind Standish. His own Colt leaped from leather and bounced in his hand. Flying metal pinned the renegade to the puncheons. He uttered a shrill peal of anguish and dropped his gun.

"Keep yore hands on the counter, friend!" Standish's voice lashed at the county clerk. Fury had crowded all gentleness out of his manner. He swung his attention back to the writhing outlaw. "Talk, blast yore dirty soul. Who gave you yore orders to kill me?"

There was agony on the man's face, but his lips twisted in a snarl of defiance.

"Why don't you find out?" he gasped.

A rising clamor of sound from the street warned Standish that the sleepy cowtown had been aroused by the shooting. In a moment men would be storming into the office and he'd be thoroughly trapped. There was feverish urgency in him, demanding that he stay and force one of these men to talk and reveal the man behind the range deviltry. But wisdom warned him there wasn't time. He whirled to the counter and dug his gun into the clerk's stomach.

"Where's my horse?" he demanded.

"The—the livery—three doors down," was the tremulous reply.

Standish turned swiftly and darted through the back room and out into the alley. Past the rear of the courthouse he raced until he swung into the yawning black exit of the livery barn.

By this time, he realized, curious townsmen would be storming into the county clerk's office. He could imagine what kind of trumped-up story the clerk would have to tell, and it would be certain to unleash the crowd's violence.

He was running through the dark corridor that separated the even row of stalls when the livery owner stepped out of the little cubbyhole that served as an office.

"What do you want, stranger?" the livery owner demanded. He was a grizzled, middle-aged man with a tart, nasal voice.

Standish gave him a rapid, cursory glance, then halted as he spotted Whitey in one of the stalls. The stallion was still saddled and whinnied in recognition at his approach. He ducked into the stall and led the animal out into the corridor.

"I've got what I want—my horse," grated Standish.

The livery owner scowled and suspicion crowded into his leathery cheeks.

"Clear out, mister. That ain't yore cayuse. A dark-haired gent with two guns brought that—"

"Yeah—I know," broke in Standish. "But Whitey's still my horse. The hombre you're talkin' about was fixin' to grab him from me."

Standish rested a hand on the horn and lifted himself into the hull. At the same moment the livery man dug for his gun.

Touching the stallion lightly with his heels, Standish sent Whitey plunging full into the older man. Whitey's powerful shoulders struck him and knocked him off his feet. Then horse and rider whirled and bolted toward the rear alley. And all the while a fresh clamor arose in the street and yelling men moved on toward the livery barn from the county clerk's office.

Standish swung into the alley. Even as he did so a small group of men who had sped out of the rear of the clerk's office, spotted him and yelled for him to halt. But Standish's only answer was to urge Whitey forward at a faster clip.

Several of the men who carried guns opened up on Standish, but their shots went wild. Then Standish was out of six-gun range, and pounding out of town, headed straight for the badlands while a few of the townsmen made a belated and half-hearted run for saddled horses.

His face grim and set, eyes narrowed by the bleak nature of his thoughts, Standish kept Whitey at a dead run until the first line of timber two miles out of New Benton shut him from view. Then he pulled the stallion in to a slower, but ground-eating canter.

And as he penetrated deeper into the badlands and the timber fell away to be replaced by towering bluffs, dry washes and arroyos, deep and treacherous ravines, he kept his eyes keened for sign of the patrolling riders he had eluded earlier in the day.

He proceeded swiftly, yet cautiously, anxious now to reach the hideout. Each passing hour—and his narrow escape from death in New Benton—had convinced him of the necessity for immediate action.

He wondered what success Jube Rockett had had in organizing his sodbuster neighbors for unified resistance against the outlaw legions. Divided, they could be wiped out one by one. But united they had a slim chance for survival. But that unity had to come swiftly, for some stirring within Standish told him the final showdown would come tonight.

Although the Legion of Vengeance had taken its first steps of active retaliation against Buchan and Runyan and was prepared to make things hot for the hooded raiders, they could not be absolutely certain whether Buchan or Randall or Brill was the man behind the range trouble.

There was no actual proof save the finding of the two dead Runyan men after the fire which had destroyed the Falling S spread—evidence which seemed to point to Chad Runyan. There was Brad Buchan's quite open attempt to frame him for rustling and his avowed urge to drive the nesters out. Last of all, Jess Hawley's tie-up with the outlaws could conceivably link Adam Brill, Hawley's friend, to the marauding raiders.

Yet, each time when Standish had been on the threshold of securing more concrete proof, circumstances had intervened to thwart his plans. At the outlaw hideout excessive renegade reinforcements and the need for getting Sally and her father out of danger had ordered a quick retreat.

Again in New Benton when the county clerk might have been induced to talk and reveal vital information, he had been forced to flee before the aroused violence of a crowd which no doubt had been informed that he, Lee Standish, was a killer and had ruthlessly attacked the two men found in the clerk's office.

Chapter Fifteen

It was near dusk when Standish arrived at the hideout. Horse and rider were caked with alkali. Whitey was streaked with sweat. Gallant and powerful as he was, he had been ridden hard this day and his sides were heaving with the strain of his labored breathing.

Ben Fuller and Lynn Boyle met Standish when he dismounted in the steep-walled canyon. Fuller's keen, penetrating eyes raked Standish's weary figure, his rigid countenance and he clucked noisily in his throat.

"One look at you, Lee, and I can tell yuh ran into trouble in New Benton," he observed sagely.

Standish's lips settled in a solid, weary line.

"Ben, you're seldom wrong," he said.

"What happened, Lee?" queried Boyle, his voice and manner filled with eager puzzlement.

"I damn near got myself killed—not to mention havin' some trouble registerin' those homestead claims for the nesters. Whoever is bossin' the outlaws isn't missin' a trick. There were armed men patrollin' the badlands this mornin'. Evidently they must have been expectin' somebody might try to get through to New Benton.

"I eluded them, all right, but they had two gunnies planted in town. They were new men and they weren't sure of me until the clerk tipped them off."

Quickly, then, Standish explained how the two men had watched him furtively, then gotten the drop on him in the county clerk's office.

"I knew you shouldn't have tried makin' the trip alone," grumbled Fuller irritably. "You take too damned many chances. You'll be no good to the Legion of Vengeance dead."

"But how did you get away?" Boyle queried while the rest of Standish's loyal crew crowded around.

They had all been toughened and hardened by their experiences of the past few days. They knew what they were up against, that their only reward for sticking with Standish might be a lonely grave in boothill, but they were fiercely loyal, bound to him by his stern righteousness, the shining example of his fierce courage and the knowledge that he would never ask them to do anything he wouldn't do himself.

"I managed to kick the Colt out of one of the jigger's hands and turn the tables on them," Standish informed Boyle. "Then I had to find Whitey again and make a run for it from the livery stable where they'd taken him."

"Looks like things are movin' to a quick conclusion," said Boyle. "If you ask me we can expect the showdown mighty soon. Better tell Lee what happened while he was gone."

"Tell me what?" Standish asked, a fresh premonition of disaster hitting him while he found himself steeling his nerves, awaiting another shock.

"Near dawn today the Drayton bank was robbed," grunted Fuller. His sun-wizened face was somber and unsmiling. "All the cash in the vault was swiped."

"The hooded raiders again?" Standish demanded.

"Looks that way." Fuller ran a gnarled hand through his thin gray hair. "If the ranchers and nesters weren't already licked, lootin' the bank just about finishes the job."

Lee Standish's eyes smoldered and his fists clenched and unclenched spasmodically.

"Adam Brill's behind that. He gutted his own bank as an excuse to close up and ruin everyone in the valley. Some of the cowmen have short-term notes that can be called in by Brill without notice, and he'll shore call them in now."

"You may be wrong," declared Fuller. "Brill was kidnapped last night, and the raiders left a note that they were takin' care of him because he tried to call in the federal law to stop the outlaws. They warned the town that any attempt to rescue Brill would serve as his death sentence and bring grief to every member of any posse that might be formed. And the town is so scared that no chase has been organized."

The news of Brill's kidnapping shook up Standish. Was it just a trick to throw suspicion away from the banker? Or was it on the level, and was Brill really paying with his life for having tried to call in federal law to stop the owlhooting?

There seemed to be no immediate or satisfactory answer to any of these questions, and the corners of Standish's long mouth turned down in a heavy curve of despair. He was bucking a blind wall. He was no nearer the discovery of the identity of the outlaw king than he had ever been.

"It's a nice kettle of fish, ain't it?" said Boyle.

Standish nodded surlily, the expression on his face tough and dismal, yet doggedly determined.

"Where do we go from here?" Fuller inquired.

Weariness was a heavy weight on Standish's shoulders. His body seemed to be one prolonged ache. He was going on nerve alone now, but that with his iron, unyielding will seemed to be enough.

"If I'm figgerin' right, the hooded raiders may try to wipe out the nester basin tonight," he murmured tersely. "If they do, they'll strike late at night when the nesters are in bed in their cabins. But their plans will hit a snag if Rockett was able to get his neighbors to round up their belongings and take refuge at his place.

"It'd be a simple matter for the renegades to swoop down on the basin and wipe out the sodbusters one by one. But if they're all in one spot, they stand a better chance of resisting attack. That attack may come tonight and I hope to catch those hooded raiders between two fires."

"Just how do we figger in the deal, Lee?" Boyle wanted to know. "Nothin' I'd like better than to burn a little powder with those hooded polecats at the other end of my slugs."

"You'll get yore chance." Standish's voice was flat-toned and almost savage in intensity. "With the nesters holin' up behind whatever cover they can find outside the cabin, we can be hidden out in the brush above the basin. If the outlaws attack, we let them get close to the cabin then close in on 'em."

"That sounds good to me," snapped Boyle. "When do we start."

"Not till later," replied Standish. "I told Rockett to be shore and advise his friends to make the shift after dark in case they're bein' watched. So, we've got some time to waste yet."

Ben Fuller rubbed his stubbled chin with a grizzled hand and glanced speculatively at his young boss.

"Such bein' the case, Lee, I'd say you'd better wrap yoreself around some chuck, then grab some shuteye. You look dog-tired."

"I haven't time to—"

"There's plenty o' time. Don't be a fool. You keep on and yuh'll keel over from exhaustion. Even two or three hours will help."

Standish grinned ruefully.

"I reckon you're right, Ben. But first, I want to take care of Whitey."

Moving to the stallion, Standish removed the saddle and blanket. Then he rubbed Whitey down, led him off through a narrow side canyon into a broad glade where the rest of the Legion horses were grazing. He let Whitey roll in the grass, and after the animal had frisked about a few minutes, he took him to a shallow creek which traversed the glade and watered him.

When he returned to the main camp he found most of the men, with the exception of the two guards stationed on top of the rocky parapet that overlooked the gulch, hunkered about a cook-fire. Lynn Boyle handed him a tin dish heaped with biscuits, beef and beans. There was strong, muddy coffee, too.

Although Standish was hungry, he was too tired to really enjoy the meal. After a few minutes he put the unfinished food down and went off to his bedroll.

It seemed that he had hardly been asleep more than a few minutes when Ben Fuller was shaking him awake.

"Gettin' late, Lee, and we've got more news," the old rannihan informed his young boss.

Standish knuckled sleep out of his eyes and stared about him. Darkness had fallen and the sky was like a black velvet carpet dotted with winking, flashing diamonds. A cool wind, faintly scented with sage, blew in from the north.

For a moment the full significance of Fuller's words did not register in his mind. But when they did, Standish leaped to his feet and gripped Fuller's shoulders with fingers that dug deeply into muscle and sinew.

"What are you sayin', Ben? Speak up!"

"That gunman of Rockett's, Ira Stone, rode up here half an hour after dark with a message from Sally, sayin' she wants yuh to meet her at Eagle's Nest at ten o'clock.

Seems she has important information for yuh." Fuller broke off and his voice dropped to a lower note. "Lee, I don't like it. There's somethin' fishy goin' on and I don't trust that gunny."

Standish appeared to consider Fuller's statement with a rigid and careful attention.

"I wonder what happened," he mused, half-aloud, a strange torment lashing his emotions.

"Lee, it's a trap," Fuller blurted, his face hard and firm. "I'll bet Sally never sent a message. If yuh ask me, Stone is workin' with the renegades unknown to Rockett. Mebbe they've kidnapped Sally, and havin' muffed their chance at New Benton, they're tryin' to lead yuh to yore doom!"

Doubt laid its brittle impression in the depths of Standish's mind. He stood still and resolute, yet his uncertainty at this moment was like a nervous hand plucking at his restraint.

"It could be a trap," he agreed slowly. "That gunsel I didn't shoot in New Benton has had plenty of time to ride to the jigger who's ramroddin' the outlawry and report his failure. This could be another attempt to cash my chips for me."

Fuller's eyes were dark with speculation, and his outthrust jaw had a challenge in it.

"What I want to know is how Stone found his way to our hideout. If those jaspers know where we've holed up, why don't they try to clean us out with guns?"

"Because there's only one entrance to our hideout—by that steep ledge trail and we command a full view of the approach," Standish told him bluntly. "We could hold off any army of men here if we had enough food and ammunition. Then again this may be on the level. The renegades may not know where we are and Sally, if she really did send a message could have told Stone how to get here, because I gave her a description of where the hideout was located last night."

Shock rolled up into Ben Fuller's face and his eyes widened.

"Lee—could—could it be possible—Sally and Rockett are runnin' a sandy against us and their neighbors?"

Sudden rage somersaulted up into Standish's features and he took a threatening step forward as his fists clenched.

"Throw that idea outa yore head, Ben," he growled. "Sally is as straight as they come and I—I—well, you're just wrong. If anyone is crooked it could be Stone and he could have easily gotten the information out of Sally. And if she and Rockett trust him—as they probably do—they'd probably talk."

Fuller's cheeks were still flushed from Standish's rebuff, but he was not angry—only with himself for saying what he had.

"Well, Stone knows where we are and if he's not on the level, we can be shore those hooded raiders know, too. And from now on when we ride outa here we'll have to be careful of running into an ambush. Lee, take my advice. Don't keep that date. It's a trap."

"But if it isn't, and Sally really has important information—or if she is in danger, I'd never forgive myself for not goin'."

"If you're set on goin', we'll ride with yuh."

"No, I've got to see this out alone," insisted Standish. "To make shore it's no trap I'll visit the Rockett place first. I'm gettin' to the bottom of this mess tonight."

Standish was thinking of Sally and wondering if she were safe. Just the thought of her, the vision of her smiling eyes and the warm red curve of her mouth was enough to quicken the blood in his veins. The depth of his feeling for her had been something strong and vital and totally beyond his control.

"But what about us, Lee?" Fuller demanded. "How do the rest of us boys figger in the deal?"

"Ben, you wait until about ten-thirty, then head for the basin with every man we've got. I want you to string them out in the brush in a big circle around the cabin. If the renegades raid tonight, let them ride right past yuh. The time to hit them will be when we've really got them outflanked."

"And where will you be?"

Standish shrugged. He made a high, square shape against the towering rock wall of the canyon. Looking at him, Fuller was impressed by the closeness of Standish's resemblance to the hard, unyielding granite at his back.

"Hard to tell where I'll be," murmured Standish. "After you've got the boys set, ride down to the cabin. If Sally's there when I arrive, I'll stay there and wait for yuh. If she's really gone—or if she's been captured by the outlaws, you might send one or two men to pick up my trail—if there is any trail—at Eagle's Nest. But no more than that, because I'm only one man. The lives of every nester may be at stake tonight. It's important they get as much protection as possible. Remember that."

Fuller nodded gloomily, the shining glint of admiration in his bleary gray eyes.

"I won't be forgettin' and the nesters better not forget, either."

Standish turned away, moved through the silent, watchful group of Legion riders and went to Whitey to saddle up.

"Sorry, Whitey boy," he murmured affectionately to the powerful stallion. "You've been ridden hard already. But there's no other horse I'd trust for tonight's work."

When he had mounted, he rode back through the camp. The men rose, tense and alert and a little apprehensive. Then he gave them a tough, humorless grin.

"Luck," said Fuller morosely.

Standish said nothing. He merely lifted his hand and rode out upon the narrow ledge trail and into the concealing darkness with his wide-shouldered body altogether stiff and straight in the saddle.

Chapter Sixteen

There was a wolfish glitter in Ace Gordon's blinking eyes as he pulled his horse to a halt at the edge of the brush behind Jube Rockett's cabin. When he saw there was no light in the place his blood began to race and sweat burst through the tightly drawn skin of his forehead.

Dismounting quickly, he left his horse ground hobbled in a thicket, and raced to the cabin. He pushed the door open, peering into the yonder gloom, then groped his way inside.

Striking a match on the seat of his levis, he moved to a coal oil lamp that set on a table and lit it. He turned the wick low, then stepped to the side and front windows and threw strips of muslin over them to keep the light from penetrating to the darkness outside.

He spent the next five minutes studying the entire expanse of floor in the main room. Then, moving aside the cot which stood against the side wall, he noted with bulging eyes a board that seemed a little looser than the others. He pried it up with an iron bar and saw a patch of dirt which had recently been disturbed.

Going to the door for the shovel he saw leaning there, he began a frenzied digging. For ten long minutes he heaved up the earth in great gobs, body tense and eager, waiting for the crunch of steel on wood or cloth that would tell him he had struck Rockett's cache of gold.

So intent was he on his work that he failed to hear the door open at his back. A slight draught of air swept into the room. It stirred the hair at the base of Gordon's neck.

It chilled a small spot between his shoulder blades. He started to turn slowly when the clink of a spur chain jerked him fully around.

"Who's that?" he shrilled, stabbing for his six-gun.

"Well, Gordon," said Lee Standish quietly, "so yuh're after gold! I reckon yuh're the jasper who took that shot at me near the basin the day I discovered Rockett at his diggings."

Gordon's pinched features grew hideous in the flickering glow of the smoke-smudged lamp.

"Shore I am," he said slowly and defiantly. "I'd seen Rockett come outa the brush a couple of times with pick and shovel, carryin' small pokes that looked as if they carried gold. That day I followed him to the creek and watched where he was workin'."

"So you were going to kill him and take the claim for yoreself," said Standish, low-voiced and intent.

"Yeah. But when I saw you I figgered I'd drill you first to—"

"To help the renegades you've been ridin' with and to doublecross yore friends," finished Standish. "I recognized yuh that night at the outlaw hideout."

Gordon's body bowed in a crouch and his lips pulled tight against his yellow teeth.

"All right, Standish," he hissed savagely. "You know so much, let's see what good it does you! I missed you once. I won't miss again!"

Gordon's arm moved in a blur of speed, his splayed fingers plucking at his low-hung gun.

"No, you don't, friend," snapped Standish thinly and launched himself across the intervening space in a headlong rush.

Gun thunder mingled with the thud of Standish's boots on the hard turf. A screaming bullet tore past his head. Then his upshooting arm slammed the smoking gun from Gordon's hand. Standish's shoulder punched into the nester, sending him backward. In the scuffle the lamp was kicked over. The glass shattered and coal oil spattered across some light kindling piled against the wall. A writhing tongue of flame, gliding with the sinuous speed of a sidewinder striking its prey, leaped up the wall, setting the cabin ablaze.

Gordon, prodded by a consuming wrath, picked up a chair and swung it toward Standish. The latter dodged, swiveling his head to one side, as a leg descended with stunning force on his shoulder. Standish felt his left arm go numb. A fist smashed against his mouth and he fell to the ground. A booted toe crashed his ribs. He rolled over, saw Gordon's crazed face with the blazing eyes filled with a raging passion to kill, saw that boot drive toward him again.

Lurching to one side, he grabbed Gordon's foot, jerked savagely and hauled the nester down beside him. He sank a feeble left into the nester's midriff, then went clawing and threshing over the earth with Gordon's thumbs probing his eyes, gouging at his windpipe.

Flames crackled and leaped about them as the fire gained headway. The red glare was all about them, lighting their faces in a lurid glow. Gordon's blinking eyes burned like fierce, bright coals.

They clawed to their feet. Standish tagged Gordon's leering face with two light left jabs, then crossed a torrid right to the chin that lifted Gordon off his feet and plunged him against the flaming cabin wall. The searing agony of the fire yanked a terrified screech from Gordon's dry throat. He grabbed up a long hunk of wood and came lunging at Standish. The rancher drifted backward.

Gordon circled, splayed mouth drooling curses, and let drive with the weapon. Standish dodged, but the blow caught him alongside the head. He tottered while a thousand red lights burst into brilliance before his eyes.

The edge of Gordon's palm sliced against his Adam's apple, sluicing the breath out of him. He choked for air and spilled on his face. Gordon jumped on him, then toppled backward with a scream as a flaming timber crashed in front of him in a shower of sparks.

Standish groaned, feeling the heat sopping up the moisture in his body. He rolled over, saw Gordon making a dash for the cabin door. Halfway across the room, the nester stumbled across the fallen chair and tripped. Standish dragged himself to his knees, then got to his feet. The flames, spurred by the draught of fresh air coming from outside, lashed across the cabin, wrapping everything in that seething, humming curtain of crimson death.

Standish reached Gordon in a desperate lunge. They traded wild blows. A knuckled fist raked Standish's mouth and blood ran warm against his grim lips. He sidestepped a wicked kick aimed at his groin, grabbed the nester's booted foot, and spilled him flat on his back.

Gordon rolled to his feet and lunged in with windmilling arms. Standish parted those wild punches, planted his own deadly blows with telling effect. Gordon's nose began to gush blood. Standish closed in, stumbled over a smoldering board as Gordon butted him cruelly. An updrawn knee smote his stomach, bringing its tumult of punishing agony.

There was a loud hiss and roar as part of the roof collapsed in the holocaust. Standish staggered blindly. Heat smote him in an intolerable wave. His groping hands encountered Gordon. A fist smashed the bridge of his nose. The pain cleared his senses. Gordon's blood-smeared face loomed close, the eyes nearly closed, face moist.

A flurry of blows pelted against Standish's cheeks like rain. He balanced on the balls of his feet, smashed that leering, blinking-eyed face with a dozen short, hard blows. He hooked a right to the stomach, then put all of his corded weight behind a pile-driving smash. The punch appeared to explode against the nester's chin with the force of a battering ram.

Gordon's mouth flew open and he disappeared behind a wall of climbing flames. Standish weaved toward the nester, then crowded backward, arms shielding his face as the blaze heaved toward him. Part of the cabin wall blew inward with a soft concussion.

Scarlet-tipped timbers fell all about him. Something hot and fiery speared across his chest. A heavy weight grazed his head and he staggered toward free air. He found the way partially blocked by the red-tinged wall that gutted the house.

In this dizzy whirl of pain and fire a feverish question hummed through his mind: Where was Sally? And where was Rockett?

Standish turned, conscious that Gordon was trapped behind a mounting crimson geyser of heat and terror. It was impossible to even attempt a rescue.

Grimly he made for the door. He lurched into the cool air. Behind him there was a soft boom. The walls of the cabin bulged and collapsed. Then thunder drummed the yard and dust churned the air as a horseman clattered up.

"Standish!" somebody yelled hoarsely.

Dimly that sound reached Lee Standish's ears. He lifted his head and saw Ira Stone, Rockett's hired gunman, riding toward him with his six-gun lifted and spewing lead. Stone's first two shots went wild as Standish reeled across the yard.

Although his gun was an immense weight in his fist, he fought desperately to bring it up. Death stared him in the face and he had the grim and terrible conviction that the next time Stone shot he would not miss. Somehow Standish brought the wavering weapon to bear upon Stone and flipped the hammer at the same moment that the roaring explosion of Stone's forty-five boxed his ears.

He was vaguely aware that Stone had missed again before the dark tide of exhaustion swept over him, plunging him into total blackness. The smoking Colt slipped from his fingers and he followed it to the ground in a headlong fall.

Chapter Seventeen

Harsh, angry voices brought Lee Standish struggling out of the pit of oblivion into which the punishing fatigue of the fight with Ace Gordon had plunged him. He was lying flat on his back and the ruddy glow from the flames of the burning cabin was gone. The only light was from several bull's-eye lanterns which showed him a closely bunched group of nesters who regarded him with a dark malevolence.

"He's comin' out of it now, Mike!" blurted Jim Holland.

A wild roar answered that statement and burly, red-cheeked Mike Carew shoved through the press of men and faced the Falling S rancher.

"It looks like us nesters were wrong once more about you, Standish," Carew informed him savagely.

Angry puzzlement rode Standish's craggy features. Long hours spent in the saddle had thinned his beard-stubbled face to the point of gauntness, carving dark hollows under his eyes, flattening his lips and increasing the toughness of his mien.

"I don't know what yuh're talkin' about," he said, clambering to his feet and swaying unsteadily.

"You know well enough!" insisted Carew, gesturing toward the blackened ruins of the Rockett cabin. "Us nesters with our families were on our way here—accordin' to Rockett's directions, suggested by you—when we saw the fire. But by the time we got here it was too late to save Rockett.

"He's dead—burned to a crisp in the ruins—and you killed him! We were fools to trust yuh. You got Rockett to believe it was best for us to hole up in one spot so's we could fight the renegades better if they attacked tonight. Now, I'm thinkin' yore idea may have been to get us in one spot so's the job o' slaughterin' us would be that much easier. Mebbe you're doublecrossin' yore own Legion of Vengeance. Where's yore men if they're supposed to be on hand to help?"

"Help who?" yelled another nester. "Us or the renegades?"

An angry murmur that rose to an ominous roar lifted through the massed group of men. Dazedly Standish glanced around, seeing the throng of people in the yard.

Rickety wagons and work horses were all over. Women and children who had joined their men in this trek to the Rockett place, huddled closely in fear. And the men, armed and driven to the end of their patience, pressed close, murder lust in their eyes.

"Yuh're crazy, Carew!" protested Standish. "That's—"

"Don't lie!" broke in Ira Stone, his hard-eyed face bleak with fierce passion. "I saw yuh stumble out of the cabin, leavin' Rockett to die there. Then yuh creased me with a slug before I could down yuh."

A kind of black remorse dropped a mask over Standish's features. Stone had a crude bandage on the top of his head, showing where his, Standish's, own labored shot had found its mark.

"Listen to me, all of yuh!" he pleaded, a fierce urgency in his tone. "The man you found in the ruins is Ace Gordon. This gunman"—and he indicated Ira Stone—"rode up to our hideout tonight and left word that Sally wanted to meet me at Eagle's Nest. Suspectin' a trap of some kind, I came here first and discovered Gordon rippin' up the floor of the cabin. I reckon he was lookin' for Rockett's gold. Gordon's in with those raiders. When he saw me he pulled a gun and we fought. The lamp overturned, a fire started and he was trapped in the blaze."

Standish finished his explanation on a rising note while a clamor of disbelief almost drowned out his words.

"You lie!" grated Mike Carew, drawing a Colt. "We looked at that body. It's charred almost beyond recognition, but it's Rockett. It's the same height and build and you killed him for the gold that only you and Rockett and myself knew about. I don't know what yore game is—whether yuh're doublecrossin' yore own Legion of Vengeance in some manner, or whether yuh just saw an easy chance to get some quick riches."

"What did yuh do with the gold?" demanded Ira Stone savagely. "It's gone. There was an empty hole in the ground where yuh probably found the gold. I'll bet Rockett surprised yuh huntin' his cache and you killed him. Yuh probably had finished hidin' the loot somewhere and was makin' shore yuh left no evidence when I rode in to queer yore game!"

Lee Standish's face turned stiff and still. The tension increased and the threat of violence was a deadly perfume in the night air.

"If the gold's gone, I don't know what became of it," he insisted. "Gordon and Rockett were the same size and build, and I tell you that's Gordon!"

"Rockett's dead," said Carew, his eyes dangerous. "Now I want to know what yuh've done with Sally before we string you up."

"Sally!" repeated Standish in a strained voice. "I don't know where she is—if she isn't here. Unless she's at Eagle's Nest. But I figgered that message Stone delivered was a trick."

"I delivered no message," snarled Stone. "Yuh've killed Rockett and now yuh've got the gal somewhere."

Standish's eyes froze into angry balls of gray ice, and his lips made a long and thin and dangerous line.

"Stone, I'd like nothin' better than to kill yuh."

"Like yuh killed Rockett?" retorted the gunman with a sneer.

Two or three other nesters pressed forward now.

"We're wastin' time here, Mike. Let's string him up and ride for those blasted masked raiders as yuh suggested before!"

Mike Carew's ruddy features turned a deeper hue, and his wide shoulders began to strain against his checkered shirt.

"It's as good a job as any. Somebody get a rope." He broke off to regard Standish with rage and scorn. "Jim Holland just got back from New Benton with two of his neighbors after dodgin' renegade patrols in the badlands. The county clerk told him that nobody had been there to file claims for our homesteads and that the government had issued a new decree declaring the basin completely free range and not open for homesteading. And you were supposed to have—"

"I filed those claims around noon today," interrupted Standish. A dark fury had its way with him, roughing up his talk. He was angry at the stubbornness and fickleness of these men who had once again turned against him on circumstantial evidence and the false testimony of a gunman who was quite obviously in the pay of the renegade gang. "That clerk is workin' with those masked raiders and tried to trap me in New Benton. I distinctly saw him make those records. He refused to give me receipts, though, and the reason is apparent."

"Shut him up, Mike, before I put a bullet through him," raged one of the other nesters. "Here's yore rope. You can see he's lying or just stallin' for time till his friends come. I'll bet that blasted Legion of Vengeance is really workin' hand in hand with the hooded raiders."

"You fools! Listen to me!" fumed Standish.

But the nesters refused to heed. They closed in on

Standish. Grimly he fought back against them, lashing out with his fists. But his efforts availed nothing against the blood-hungry mob, and he was overpowered quickly by the sheer weight of numbers.

Someone slipped a noose about his neck and he was dragged past the smoking ruins of the cabin to a slight knoll covered by two cottonwoods. Like a candle snuffed out by the wind, hope vanished within him and his mind plumbed the depths of despair.

After he had been hoisted aboard his horse Ira Stone threw the free end of the rope across a low branch of the tree.

Waiting for the solid, biting crunch of hempen strands into his neck, Standish stiffened when a hoarse cry pierced the night. He saw Carew and Stone and the other nesters turn around, heard the gasps of astonishment that burst from several throats. Then he heard the rumble of wheels and saw a rickety flatbed wagon lurch up the slope. There was a man at the reins, swaying weakly as he tried to bring the team to a halt, and the man was Jube Rockett!

Jim Holland and Mike Carew ran alongside the bays, gripped the reins and brought them to a halt. Then as Rockett lurched to one side and seemed about to pitch from the seat, other nesters ran forward to catch him and help him to the ground.

He had been shot. Blood bathed the top of his shirt. Already wounded in the side in the shooting fray at the outlaw hideout, Rockett had now stopped another bullet. Weakness threatened to plunge him into unconsciousness, but he fought to rally his flagging energy.

"Jube! We thought you were dead!" blurted Mike Carew, leading Rockett to the knoll where Standish was under guard. "Yore place burned down and we found a charred body we took to be you."

"Raiders again?" Rockett gasped.

"No," replied Carew. "There was a fight. Standish said it was between him and Ace Gordon, but we thought he was lyin'."

Suddenly Rockett noticed Standish.

"What are you tryin' to do to him?" the nester demanded.

"We were goin' to hang him for killin' you and stealin' the gold you spoke about last night."

Briefly Carew gave an account of what had occurred in the basin, faithfully repeating Standish's version of the affair. When he had finished Rockett straightened, grimacing in pain.

"Take that rope off his neck! Mike, you should have known better. As for the gold, I took it out of the cabin and cached it up in the brush."

Hands that had been eager to hang Standish a moment before now hurried to remove the noose. Relief was like a wild, sweet pain flooding his veins and breaking down the tight constriction around his heart.

"But what about those homestead claims?" insisted Ira Stone.

At Rockett's questioning look the gunman recounted Jim Holland's experience at New Benton. Then Standish broke in gruffly.

"I'm sorry about the cabin, Jube. It couldn't be helped. I caught Gordon huntin' for yore gold and we fought. He admitted he was with the renegades. He was the jasper who tried to drygulch us near yore diggings.

"As for those claims, the county clerk was bribed by the outlaws to play ball with 'em. He probably destroyed those records right after he made them. Only thing to do now is to organize and hunt those outlaws without any waste of time." He broke to ask abruptly: "Where's Sally?"

Rockett was a tired old man, weary in body and soul,

with a new weight of fear and hopelessness dragging at his nerves.

"The raiders got her," he said tightly. "I hurried back here for help after—well, I'll start from the beginnin'.

"Sally rode into Drayton with me for supplies. I figgered if we were goin' to fight we'd need food and ammunition. On the way back a bunch of those owlhooters blocked up the trail. They ordered me to stop. I lost my head and whipped up the team, shooting as I went. One of the jaspers drilled me in the shoulder and I fell off the wagon.

"When I came to I saw that the team had stopped about fifty yards away. The raiders were gone and so was Sally and most of my supplies. They left this note for me. I reckon they made shore I wasn't dead before they vamosed."

Silently he passed a jagged piece of paper to Standish.

"What does it say?" demanded Carew.

Standish's eyelids crept down over somber gray eyes in which stark menace was wickedly flaming.

"It says," his flat-toned voice murmured, "that if Rockett wants to see Sally alive again he's got three hours to get outa Drayton. If he obeys Sally will be returned unharmed to New Benton in two days. If he does not, she'll die. And there's an added warning that unless all nesters leave with Rockett the entire basin will be burned out."

"The dirty blackguards!" breathed Mike Carew.

"There's somethin' else," blurted Rockett. "My shootin' from the buckboard was bad, but I downed one hombre's horse. It was carryin' the AB Connected brand on its rump."

"That's Adam Brill!" snapped Lee Standish with a fierce intensity. "He's our man! I've thought so from the moment we got Jess Hawley to talk. Brill's the gent behind those raids and it's time we smashed him. If he has Sally I'll follow him clear to hades and back to get her."

The booming rataplan of hoofs sounded along the slope in back of the smoking ruins of Rockett's cabin. Nesters swung about, hands dropping to rifles or six-guns as a band of horsemen swept into view. Then those hands relaxed as Ben Fuller's voice announced their identity.

"We were on our way to the basin, when we saw the fire. We figgered somethin' had gone wrong, so we rushed right here instead of stayin' in the brush," explained Fuller, skidding his mount to a halt at the head of the Legion of Vengeance. "Lee, you're okay?"

"Yeah," said Standish dryly. "Except for almost gettin' roasted alive, then bein' hung in the bargain." He didn't bother to elaborate when Fuller's eyebrows elevated questioningly. "You boys are just in time for war.

"The raiders have Sally Rockett. We aim to get her back and smash that gang at the same time. They just jumped Rockett and Sally on the way from town with supplies. Rockett nailed one of their horses and it was carryin' Brill's AB Connected brand. Here, read this."

Fuller glanced at the message Standish held out to him.

"Let's ride," snapped Fuller. "What are we waitin' for?"

Ira Stone made a move toward his horse with the others, but Standish stopped him.

"Not you, Stone. You're stayin' here. Deliverin' that fake message from Sally proves yuh're with the renegades." Standish gestured to Jim Holland and another man. "Holland, suppose you, McGready and a few others keep guard over Stone and the women and children till we return."

Holland, never a man for a fight, agreed with alacrity as did his neighbor. Then while Stone cursed harshly, his guns were removed and the others rode off.

As the Legion of Vengeance struck off through the

brush Standish leaned over in his saddle and yelled to Fuller.

"If Brill and the raiders are at the AB Connected, I figger we'll find Runyan and mebbe Buchan with him," he intoned.

"Why Buchan?" inquired Fuller.

"Because he framed me for that cattle theft. He's in it and so is Runyan. Findin' those two Double R men at the Falling S proved that."

They had gone a quarter mile when Fuller hipped about in the saddle and gestured with his arm.

"There's a fire!" he roared. "Looks like the Circle B. If Buchan's with Brill in those raids you figger he'd be burnin' his own spread?"

Standish stared across the rolling country where a red glow was gashing a ragged hole out of the night.

"It's the Circle B, all right," he agreed. "I still think Buchan is with the renegades. Mebbe those raiders operated in two or three separate bunches. Brill had one gang of paid gunslicks. Buchan's entire Circle B made another outfit, and Runyan's crew a third. This fire may be Brill's way of playin' the game whole hog, to smash Buchan and leave the way clear for himself."

Chapter Eighteen

On and on through the night they raced like a horde of dark, avenging ghosts. And all the time the glow in the sky grew redder and more brilliant. They heard no sounds of gunshots and met no other riders. Then, when they were close to the ranch buildings and the fire began to wane, Standish turned and spoke to Fuller.

"Somethin' tells me this is the night set by the raiders for takin' over the whole range."

Without any attempt at caution they stormed into the Circle B ranchyard and found it deserted save for the dark bulk of sprawled bodies on the ground and one or two riderless horses. Flames had gutted all the buildings, leaving them gaunt skeletons in which the livid lace work of fire tongues still danced feebly in reddish hunger.

"The Circle B is wiped out!" blurted Mike Carew.

Most of the men remained in their saddles, trying to curb their impatient horses. But Standish, Fuller, Boyle and Carew climbed down to identify the bodies. When they had finished Standish's face carried a rough, untamed look in which determination burned more fiercely than ever.

"Six of those men were regular Circle B hands," he said. "They all had black hoods inside their shirts. The other three were *wearing* their hoods, and they're gunslicks *I never saw before.*"

"What do you make of it?" Lynn Boyle asked.

"Just like I said before. The fact that three are strangers and wearing hoods convinces me they're part of a bunch who attempted to wipe out Buchan tonight. I'll wager that Buchan served his usefulness and this was his reward from Brill."

They hit their saddles again and continued on at the same relentless pace. This time they had barely covered two miles when they saw another reddish glow in the sky and heard the distant clatter of guns.

"That's comin' from Chad Runyan's Double R. not far from the AB Connected!" Standish's voice lifted stridently above the pound of hoofs. "It's all fallin' into a pattern. First the Circle B, now the Double R. If Runyan was with the raiders, as I figger, then he, too, is bein' smashed now that he's served his purpose. It's one big doublecross."

Slamming to a halt atop a low ridge the Legionnaires saw the Double R ranch sprawled in a brushchoked glade. The barn was afire, but the other buildings were still intact. Gun flashes stabbed out of ranchhouse and bunkhouse windows, while outside yelling horsemen surged in a huge circle, pouring a hail of lead at the defenders.

"Let's pitch in!" said Standish.

With a wild roar of approval the Legion of Vengeance thundered down the slope, every man unlimbering his gun, preparing it for action. They rode bunched up for several hundred yards, studying the terrain.

Most of the horsemen in the glade wore black hoods. But at the edge of the galloping circle of riders was another ring of unmasked men. It was evident that this outer fringe was firing at the hooded men, as were the defenders of the ranch buildings. Noticing that, Standish lifted his hand for the party to slow up. Even as he did so the strident voice of Brad Buchan boomed during a lull in the firing.

"Brill, you dirty skunk! You doublecrossed us. The Circle B did yore dirty work so you burned us out. You left six of my men dead back there, but we've come to pay yuh back!"

Someone yelled fiercely in return, then a fresh hail of lead washed across the night. But the Circle B waddies were on the move and they answered that blast with a wicked volley of their own.

"We're cleanin' you and yore picked gunnies out, Brill!" blared Buchan. "And then we're smashin' Runyan and the nesters! Come on, you Circle B hellions, give those sidewinders the devil!"

Instantly the battle was renewed in a rising crescendo of sound. Men fought their mounts in milling circles, flame stabbing from their guns.

"You all heard that!" snapped Standish. "The skunks are fightin' among themselves! We'll concentrate on those masked raiders caught in the center, then hit the Circle B outfit. After that we'll give Runyan a chance to surrender. If he refuses, it'll be fight to the finish."

He raised his arm and the Legion riders put spurs to their mounts and bolted down the grade. They saw scattered Circle B men whirl their horses and start shooting wildly.

"This is showdown, Buchan and Brill!" Standish thundered. "The Legion of Vengeance is payin' off all debts in lead tonight!"

The only answer was a storm of flying metal that buzzed past Legion faces. They were in the midst of the conflict and their guns added to the unholy din. Smoke drifted back and forth across the glade, and it was punctuated by vivid orange flashes, the yammering of six-guns.

Two hooded riders bolted toward Standish, their .45s gouging crimson holes in the gloom. He felt the hot breath of bullets speeding past his cheeks. His ivory-handled Colt steadied, then bucked against his wrist. He heard a man's agonized yell, then a horse pitched toward Whitey.

A waxen face, ghastly with pain and fear, loomed close to him. There was a crazed light in the man's eyes, a hideous hole in his throat. Then he was gone, plunging into eternity. Standish raced on grimly.

Chaos reigned in the glade. Outlaws caught in a terrible crossfire of spitting guns were tossed from their panic-stricken mounts and trampled underfoot. The Double R punchers were keeping up a withering fire from the ranch buildings.

Yet, there seemed to be no end to the huge band of hooded raiders which circled the buildings, firing as they rode. Others of the masked men were battling the remnants of the Circle B as well as the recklessly charging Legion of Vengeance.

Suddenly out of that welter of horses and men Standish glimpsed the tall, powerful figure of Brad Buchan.

"Buchan! Let 'er flame!" he yelled stridently.

He saw the Circle B owner twist about in the saddle. The latter's gun came up, ready to squeeze out a shot. But then Buchan curveted away, intent upon a bulky rider covered by a black hood. Afterward, Standish heard Buchan's outraged voice.

"Brill! Turn around and take this lead for yore belly!"

The bulky figure in the saddle never wavered in its headlong flight across the glade. Standish saw muzzle light flicker between the two men. Then Buchan half-lifted out of the saddle, clamping a hand to his shoulder. Grimly he fired at the hooded figure and missed.

Buchan's horse was shot out from under him and he arched over the animal's head in a flying leap. Standish hopped about, his six-gun spewing lead at the fleeing hooded figure, but without effect. Gun-flame flickered toward him. Whitey faltered as a bullet struck a vital spot. Abruptly Standish found himself flying through space.

He landed on his shoulder to the sound of feverish cursing not far away. He saw the hooded rider making good his escape. Certain now that the man was Brill, Standish wondered with an odd, numbing fear what had become of Sally.

"All right, Standish. You asked for it!"

It was Brad Buchan talking and his features were a mask of killing rage. He fired once wildly, the bullet smashing into a tree behind Standish. The latter rolled to his knees. His thumb snapped the hammer and the explosion of the shot ripped out.

"Blast you—Standish—" Buchan gasped hoarsely.

Then the Circle B owner began to wilt and tremble. Grayness came to his cheeks and blood flecked his lips as he fell forward on his face. Grimly Standish hauled himself to a low crouch. Riders were pounding back and forth and he was caught in a crossfire himself. At any moment death might mark him with its stern, implacable hand.

But he was past caring about that. His blood raced with the frenzy of combat. There was no mercy in him, and he was as hard and resolute as any man had ever been. His eyes sought that bulky, hooded rider. The moonlight etched the dark figure halfway up a steep slope with another horseman beside him. Both men were evidently headed in the direction of the AB Connected, and Standish realized Brill was playing the game safe.

Brill must have seen that this battle could have but one disastrous end for his raiders. Accordingly, just as a slinking rat deserts a sinking ship, so Brill was abandoning his men. And if he were bound for his ranch, then Sally must be there. With his organization of crime smashed, Brill would use the girl as a hostage to get safely out of the country.

That thought sent ice rippling through Standish's veins and he lurched through the shrouding smoke toward a riderless horse. At once another rider pounded out of the shadows and crashed against him. A gun glinted in a fleck of moonlight, then Ben Fuller's voice reached him.

"Lee, I darned near plugged yuh," he gasped. "They get Whitey?"

"Yeah," Standish gasped. "Ben, give me yore horse. Think I saw Brill and another rider head for the AB Connected. I'm shore they've got Sally somewhere and I aim to get her or die tryin'."

"I'll go along."

"No. You stay here to direct this fight. It's turnin' into a slaughter. Somehow it's got to be stopped. Concentrate on those hooded men. Don't fire on Runyan. He may be with the skunks, too, as I figger, but make shore before the issue is forced."

Fuller came out of the saddle. Standish mounted and whirled the dark gelding straight toward the steep side trail in the timber. Bullets combed the air, questing for him with greedy, scarlet-tipped fingers. But somehow he rode the gauntlet safely.

Fifteen minutes later the lights of the small AB Connected ranchhouse flashed up before him. He proceeded to the edge of the brush at a headlong pace, then leaped off the gelding. There were three horses tethered at the side of the house. But he was so tormented by fears for Sally, that he paid it no special attention.

Standish crept to the veranda, tiptoed across it. His hand fastened on the door, then flung it open. Even as he did so he heard a slight scuffing sound. But he forgot about it when he plunged into the room and saw Sally's white, haunted face staring at him from a big chair.

The girl had been securely trussed in it, but was now free, the ropes lying at the foot of the chair.

"Lee! I knew you'd come!" she cried.

Adam Brill, the black hood he had worn tossed carelessly on the floor, whirled from an open safe from which he was taking stacked piles of money and stuffing them into a bag. There was nothing gentle in his eyes, which gleamed like the tawny orbs of a panther. And there was nothing gentle in the way his lips pulled back against his teeth.

Yet fear made an ugly track across his flabby cheeks when his glance went to Lee Standish's craggy face which was gaunter and tougher and more implacable than anything the banker had ever seen.

"Trail's end for you, Brill!" he murmured, his gun coming up. "Yuh're the skunk behind those raiders, and I'm gutshootin' you for all the men yuh sent to their deaths."

For a moment fear lingered in Brill's eyes, then a shrewd cunning turned them brighter, more savage. He leaped to one side, hand streaking inside his frock coat at the same moment that Sally looked beyond Standish and cried out in a heart-choking frenzy.

"Behind you, Lee!"

Standish pivoted, all his muscles going loose. Through the doorway charged the sneering, triumphant figure of Kip Randall, Buchan's ramrod. In a flashing moment of bitterness Standish cursed at his own carelessness in forgetting that Brill had ridden here with another man. And Randall's presence probably signified that he was working closely with Brill and had helped doublecross his own boss.

Chapter Nineteen

Now he was caught between a deadly crossfire and his chances of survival were slim. They had him hemmed in—a target for their glittering hatred and their gleaming guns. Even as he leaped to one side, trying to center his Colt upon Randall, the latter's gun exploded, spewing its livid flame streak toward the Falling S rancher.

Instantly a hot iron seemed to be laid along Standish's right shoulder blade. The shock of that blow sent a horrible numbness seeping along the sinews of his arm. He couldn't lift his gun-hand for a shot. Desperately he transferred the weapon to his left hand.

He had done a little southpaw shooting, but not enough to assure any sort of accuracy even at a short distance unless he took his time. And now he knew that he'd have to take his time, even though a slug from Randall's or Brill's gun burned him down.

Out of the tail of his eye he saw Brill move forward, murder in every gesture. Then Sally flung herself upon the bulky banker, grappling with him. She cried out when he struck her with the flat of his hand. But she hung on, her fingers flailing his cheeks, then seeking to get a grip on the hand that held the gun.

Standish noted all that in a fleeting clock-tick of time before his attention whirled back to Randall whose gun was centering upon him for a finishing shot. Punishing pain made the room reel around before Standish's narrowed eyes. There was a terrific buzzing roar in his head and Randall was only a misty, uncertain wraith in his vision. His left hand rose slowly and it took an age to steady the barrel, line the sights upon Randall's chest.

Another explosion shook the walls of the room. Ruddy flame hosed toward Standish. But somehow haste made Randall miss and a horneting slug dug into the plaster behind the Falling S rancher. Then his own Colt boomed and he saw a look of incredulous amazement spread over Randall's swarthy features. Slowly that look gave way to one of graying deathly pallor. His knees unhinged while his splayed fingers acted as a sieve for the scarlet trickles of blood seeping out of a mortal wound in his chest.

Behind him Standish heard a savage bellow of rage, then the sharp *thock* of a fist meeting flesh and bone. He whirled swiftly, lost his balance and fell to his knees while a slug from Brill's Colt bored over his head. Sally, propelled by the force of the banker's wicked blow, reeled against a chair, slid along its side and toppled to the floor.

Rage made its hot, feverish tumult in Standish's veins while death closed in on the smoke-shrouded air of the room. Standish's gun came up awkwardly. He dropped the hammer and felt his blood run cold when the spur clicked down on an empty cylinder.

Adam Brill laughed harshly and triumphantly.

"This is yore finish, Standish!" he yelled and fired.

But Standish was lunging forward in a low dive, the six-gun hurtling from his hand. Flying metal surged past Standish and the bursting powder flash blinded him momentarily. He saw his weapon strike the banker in the face, then he was hitting Brill at the knees with all the power in his good shoulder, driving the man backward.

Brill chopped off another wild shot as he lost his balance. Standish's weight bore him down and there was a sickening thud when Brill's skull collided with the sharp edge of the table near him. Both men hit the floor with a solid, jarring bounce and Brill went limp.

Through what seemed long ages of time Lee Standish climbed to his feet and took two staggering steps across the room. He was a thoroughly beaten man at this moment. His spent, weary body had reached the end of its endurance. He had fought and battled until the last reserves of his energy, of his indomitable will had been exhausted.

Darkness started to crowd in over his mind. He shook his head, unaware that he was falling until soft arms came around him and a husky voice murmured plaintively near his ear.

"Lee, my darling!"

He twisted his head, conscious that this was Sally beside him and that he ought to smile at her. He heard the ragged run of her breathing, caught the subtle perfume of her hair before he collapsed in a chair, almost carrying the girl to the floor.

He must have gone out, for something cold and wet brought his eyes open, shook him back to a world of reality. There were hoofbeats in the yard. Men were stridently yelling and lumbering into the room.

"Lee! I thought yuh were done for!"

That was Ben Fuller's voice and it filled Standish with a warm feeling of relief. But for the moment his attention swung away from Fuller. His eyes slid down to his bared shoulder. With an amazed start he noticed a crude, slightly bloody bandage. And there was something cool and moist on his forehead.

It was a wet compress that Sally was holding against his brow. Now color flushed her cheeks and her eyes turned misty and shiny when he shifted slightly to look at her.

"Then I'm still here?" he queried huskily.

"Oh, darling, yes!" she breathed, her arms going

around him with a hard possessiveness. "But I—I wasn't sure. I thought—"

She broke off and Standish knew in what direction her thoughts had fled. He smiled and gently pushed her away while he watched the battle-scarred men who filed into the room. Ben Fuller had led the crowd. Now Lynn Boyle, Mike Carew and Chad Runyan came in, followed by other Falling S and Double R punchers.

"Looks like yuh got here just in time to keep Brill from hightailin' with all his dough and with Sally," said Mike Carew.

Standish nodded somberly, his face still stern.

"Yeah. It was a near thing," he said, thinking more of Sally than of anything else. Then he gestured at the open safe, the strewn currency. "From the looks of all that money I'd say Brill had the bank robbed and faked his kidnapping by his own outlaws to direct suspicion away from him and make shore he ruined us all."

"That's plain enough," acknowledged Carew.

The keen, compelling intensity of Chad Runyan's gaze drew Lee Standish's attention.

"That fight at the Double R. It's over?" he asked Fuller.

"All finished," replied Fuller, nursing a bullet-broken arm, yet grinning through his obvious discomfort. "The renegades are smashed. Those we didn't kill or capture are rattlin' their hocks plumb outa the country."

"And what about you, Runyan?"

The gravity left Chad Runyan's features and his mouth quirked.

"I reckon my boys were all set to let go against yore Legion of Vengeance, figgerin' yuh were with the renegades. But after we saw how they were droppin' those masked hombres in their tracks I somehow got the idea mebbe I'd been mistaken.

"When those hooded men had been routed and my

Double R crew was still holed up in the house, Fuller ordered us all out to surrender, sayin' we'd get the same dose as the other renegades unless we did. Then Sheriff Manders backed him up and I began to believe you were fightin' on the right side."

"Yeah, but we had one heck of a time convincin' Manders and Fuller that *we* weren't in the wrong," added a wounded Double R puncher.

"That's right," agreed Runyan. "But we finally ironed out things with the help of Manders. I never did think much of you as a lawman—you played politics too much, Syl"—the rancher added, looking at Manders—"but I never knew yuh to lie and some of the things yuh told me about Brill and Buchan and yore bein' held a prisoner by Brill sorta open my eyes."

Manders flushed uncomfortably, but faced Runyan.

"I deserved that, I reckon. I ain't been much of a lawman, but seein' Standish battle with a handful of men to preserve this range has made me feel ashamed. That's why I joined in after his men rescued me from the outlaw hideout."

"Yuh're shore of Runyan, Syl?" demanded Standish, his face unrelenting. "I ain't forgettin' them two Double R punchers that were killed in that raid on the Falling S."

Chad Runyan broke in hastily before Manders could answer.

"I don't blame yuh for bein' suspicious, Lee," he said. "But I can assure you that those two men of mine you found were not workin' with the renegades under my orders. They were on their own."

Standish watched Runyan for a long, silent moment and there was no denying the man's sincerity.

"That's right, Lee," added Fuller. "We found two more Runyan waddies with those masked renegades, not to mention a few crooked gents from John Noonan's outfit in the hills. Those outlaws had spies with every ranch, I reckon. As for the rest of the skunks—they were paid gunslicks and total strangers to this country."

Standish nodded, the edge leaving his voice.

"I guess we're even, Chad. You suspected me, and I suspected you. Sorry about that Double R herd we scattered in the badlands."

"Forget it. We'll round the critters up next week."

"Say, Brill's comin' out of it!" yelled Lynn Boyle.

"Good," said Standish grimly. "Mebbe he'll live to hang for all the death and misery he caused. What about Brad Buchan?"

"He's still livin'," replied Fuller. "We left him under guard. He don't want to die and he don't want to hang, so he talked, tellin' all he knew."

"He kept cursin' Brill for doublecrossin' him," informed Runyan. "He admitted they were in the deal together to grab all the range and that his job had been to drive out the nesters and smash you, Lee.

"Brill even bought the clerk at New Benton, payin' him to destroy the record of claims you filed with him and to tell any of the nesters who might inquire that you hadn't been there and that the government had closed the basin to homesteading. But he kept mumblin' about not knowin' what was really behind it."

Standish grimaced in pain and weariness.

"Brill played it real cagey, then, because the big thing behind this land grab was that new spur the railroad plans to build from New Benton to Drayton. We found out about it from Jess Hawley, who is really a railroad agent, after we kidnapped him from the owlhooters' hideout."

Speaking tersely, Standish went on to outline the details of the clever plan which Adam Brill had engineered for complete domination of the valley.

"It's all over now," Runyan murmured somberly. "A lot of men had to die because of Brill's unholy greed, but I've a feeling things will be better. That spur will triple the value of our land. We'll get a fair price from the road for anything we have to sell, and the coming of the railroad will simplify our cattle shipping problems, bring business to the town."

"And if this war has done anything it should have taught cowmen and nesters alike that there's room enough in Drayton for everyone to live peacefully," said Standish with a determination and a fervor that made every man in the room look closely at him. "How about that, Carew, and you, Chad?"

"I agree," said ruddy-cheeked Mike Carew with alacrity. "Speakin' for my neighbors. I can say I've got no fight with the cattlemen."

"That goes for me," murmured Runyan. "I admit I haven't liked you fellows living in the basin, and I admit I was in favor of drivin' you out by force. But I was wrong."

The heavy lump of bitterness that had lain like a great weight inside Lee Standish these last few days began to dissolve.

"I'm glad to hear you both say that," he declared. He looked at Sally and she smiled at him, taking his right hand in her two slender hands. "There's hard work ahead for all of us these next few weeks, but it will be worth it. The bank will have to be reorganized and we may have to pool what little money we have to get it going again, even after the money Brill stole is returned.

"Carew, you and Rockett and the others can file yore claims legally in New Benton the first chance you get to safeguard yore holdings. As for me, I reckon I'll have to rebuild my ranchhouse."

Chad Runyan and Mike Carew nodded. They glanced toward Sally and Standish. Something in the fierce way she looked at the men startled them until Runyan smiled and nudged Carew. The nester smiled, too, and started toward the door, followed by the others.

"We sent for Doc Parker and Doc Modern," said Runyan over his shoulder. "From the looks of you I reckon you could stand some patchin'."

But Standish didn't hear him, nor did Sally, for she was watching him with a close, half-frowning glance.

"You really need a new ranchhouse," she said, a strange emphasis in her words.

Standish's head lifted and his eyes met hers. He felt the softness and the warmth of her body, the pounding surge of her heart. Her glowing eyes were intimate and filled with a rich promise. At this moment a quiet serenity, a strange sense of contentment came to this man whose life had been a succession of dangerous risks.

"And I need something else, Sally," he murmured. "If I build that ranchhouse, I'll need someone to hang the curtains—someone like you. Do you think you'd like that?"

He was smiling now and it did something to the gaunt taciturnity of his cheeks. Pain and exhaustion had thinned his features, tightened his nerves. But now the smile was softening the hard lines trouble had etched there.

"I'd love it, Lee—darling!" Sally cried, happiness leaping up into her eyes.

Standish brought her to him with a rough sweep of his arms even though the action sent fresh agony throbbing up through his shoulder. The sudden warm and yielding pressure of her lips filled him with a wild tumult he had never known.

Here they were—one man and one woman, torn and battered by a range war which had left its grim mark upon them.

It would color their lives and actions in the days to come. But out of that chaos had emerged a greater peace and a greater contentment for the people who had weathered the storm. From this moment on life would begin again.

And looking at Sally, smiling and happy in his arms, Lee Standish knew that the battle had not been in vain. He forgot his pain and the bitterness of dark memories and with this girl beside him he would look toward new horizons—a new and better tomorrow.